BLOOD HERETICS

Books by Martin Wilsey

Solstice 31 Trilogy

Still Falling
The Broken Cage
Blood of the Scarecrow

Solstice 31 Universe

Virtues of the Vicious
Shadows of the Sentinel
The Law of Lumina

The Vampire Conspiracy

Blood Heretics
Blood Sky Dreams *

Short Story Collections

Six Years Out

Anthologies as Editor

Silence of the Apoc
Whispers of the Apoc
The Witness Paradox

** forthcoming*

BLOOD HERETICS

MARTIN WILSEY

Tannhauser Press

Blood Heretics

v1.0

Paperback ISBN: 979-8-89719-032-4
Hardcover ISBN: 978-1-945994-86-9

Urban Tribe, a font from Jonathan Swinn,
Licensed for commercial use.

Banker Square, a font from FontSite Inc.,
free for commercial and personal use.

Published by Tannhauser Press
www.tannhauserpress.com

Cover created by Virtual Designs
Edited by Donna Royston
Interior Design by David Keener

For Chris Schwartz.
Because he never got to read it.

RIP

CONTENTS

HUNTER TEAM

Command and Support

Beeker	*Robert Ianni.* Lab technician and forensic scientist.
Coffee	*Rodney Jones.* Tech whiz; runs on coffee and donuts.
Hook	*Dr. Franklin.* The team's medical doctor.
Six	*Trevor Sloan.* Operations Chief, and the founding member of the team.

Tactical Team

Book	*Dan Hood.* Hunter and researcher.
Brick	*Joseph Coyle.* Hunter and researcher.
Chan	*Charles Weston.* Named after Charlie Chan.
Crash	*Herbert Nims.* Ex-Army, now a hunter.
Gram	*Diana Aubrey.* Armorer and weapons expert.
Oddjob	*Jim Whitecloud.* Taciturn hunter of Native American descent. A founding member.
Shack	*Philip Barns.* Hunter, Tech Specialist.
Snow	*Yuki Takahashi.* Female helicopter pilot and sniper, formerly Coast Guard.
~~**Switch**~~	*Daniel Rawn,* deceased. Functioned as a "loose cannon," a troubleshooter for the team.
Tank	*Mike Tanner.* Surveillance specialist. "cam guy."

Recruits, Tactical Team

–	*Timothy Beck.* A former priest with a new vocation; also a replacement for Switch.
–	*Maris Hodge.* Newest recruit. Ex-police.

1. BECK ARRIVES

Father Beck closed the disturbing file and returned it to his briefcase with all the others. He waited patiently for the other passengers to disembark, trying to calm his heart before he rose from his seat to collect his bag from the overhead. The flight from Dallas to New York seemed to take far too long. The conversation he'd had with the woman seated next to him seemed unreal somehow. They'd talked about the weather and the chance to see snow again. He'd told her about his mission work at an orphanage outside Mexico City. She'd told him about her grandchildren.

It was all so normal, though nothing was normal anymore.

If she had any idea what he'd been thinking during their conversation, she'd grab her daughter and grandchildren and take them out of the city that instant.

Or think I'm insane.

The hall leading from the plane to the gate entrance gave the illusion of descending a shaft. It unnerved him. He hadn't been off the plane for ten seconds and could already hear his heart beating.

The black and white collar he wore, which had always been so comfortable since the day he first put it on, seemed tight, constricting. He thought he'd miss wearing it when they told him he wouldn't be able to. Now, all he wanted to do was get out of it. The feeling of crosshairs on his neck seemed to focus on the collar. He hadn't felt that since Iraq. Since the day he'd decided to become a priest.

He bypassed the baggage claim and went directly to the passenger pickup area. He didn't own anything needing a bag larger than his carry-on. He'd been told everything would be provided for him once he reached New York.

For the thousandth time, he wondered what these people would be like. He knew the man named Jim Whitehorse, call sign Oddjob, would pick him up. He was there as soon as the automatic doors slid open to a blast of cold winter air. Beck recognized him from the picture in his file. He stood out from all the other people around him by both his size and stoic demeanor. Oddjob identified himself in a perfect military fashion. "Father Beck, my name is Oddjob. This way, please." Then Oddjob turned on his heels without any other greeting or preamble and walked to a rusty gray, nondescript Chevy Blazer waiting at the curb beneath a harsh halogen street lamp. He was a very muscular man dressed in Levi's, high tops, a well-broken-in leather coat, a Yankees baseball cap, and a neck too thick for his head. Oddjob's manner exuded confidence amplified by his physical size—a complete professional. Father Beck suffered the momentary memory of watching many men like this die a lifetime ago.

The priest opened the front door, tossed his bag and briefcase in the back seat, and climbed into the truck without a word. He couldn't help but notice that this was as serious as he'd been led to believe. The Blazer had dark-tinted windows and was full of high-tech communications equipment of all kinds. The truck's center console had a rack holding a pair of riot shotguns. Oddjob drew from a breast pocket a cell phone and touched the autodial number one. "Beck is in," was all he said. Then, after a moment, without a further word, he hung up the phone and pulled away from the curb.

The air was cold and crisp. A light dusting of new snow made the city look clean. It all increased the feeling of unreality. All the training, all the briefs, all the videos, all the reports were becoming a reality here.

There were vampires in this city.

***

The Blazer seemed to navigate the city streets of its own volition. Oddjob had an economy of movement, making it seem he was hardly there. Beck had become completely lost before they turned into an alley that opened to an expansive courtyard between lightless, old brick buildings. They pulled up beside a tractor-trailer that said "Entenmann's Bakery" and advertised its non-fat, no-cholesterol pound cake. Oddjob hadn't uttered another word on the ride through the city. Father Beck knew their general direction, though he hadn't been to New York in several years. Oddjob didn't seem like the type prone to small talk, so they'd ridden in silence. The Entenmann's truck was parked on the fringe of Greenwich Village, inconspicuously tucked away.

Father Beck collected his bag and got out of the truck. Oddjob made no move to get out or leave. The priest remembered the type, the eternal patience, the ready on standby, and wondered what he thought as he rounded the back of the trailer. Portable stairs led up to a door in the back that was in the process of opening. A bright, smiling face greeted him as he reached the top of the stairs and entered the trailer.

"Father Beck, good to finally meet you."

Beck recognized the man as the operations chief, Trevor Sloan, and was instantly taken in by the man's quick smile and friendly nature. According to the reports, Sloan could keep his sense of humor in the most adverse conditions: "The man redefines the term *grace under pressure*," one of the reports stated. They entered a small room at the back of the trailer. There were closets on each side, and on the walls were coat hooks with a half dozen coats. Some galoshes sat drying on a mat. Beck dropped his bag on a bench beneath the hooks and followed Sloan into the next room through a heavy steel door. The sound of the Blazer starting could be heard faintly through the trailer walls.

"Mind if I call you Tim? Not that it will matter much. You'll probably have a nickname before the month is out. Nobody's "Father" around here either, but seeing you're still in uniform tonight..." he trailed off as they entered the next room. Something seemed to be happening. The room, which took the middle twenty feet of the trailer, looked like the inside of a TV station control room. Color monitors with various scenes covered the walls. Four chairs were occupied by men, intent on their station's functions. A large screen monitor occupied most of the wall opposite where Father Beck stood—the message "FULL ALERT" pulsed in red at the bottom left of the screen. The quiet was intense.

The image on the main viewer was green monochrome with very high contrast. A man stood motionless in a doorway of an old brownstone-type building. The flatness of the image and the complete lack of shadows indicated to Beck that he was looking at a scene via infrared, which was in complete darkness.

I'm here three minutes, and I see my first vampire! Beck thought.

Sloan reached over the nearest man's shoulder, picked up a wireless headset, and put it on, speaking into the small mic before it was settled in place.

"Coffee, give me a status," Sloan barked. Beck realized "Coffee" was the man's name at the farthest station.

"All stations, standing by," one man replied.

"ETA eight minutes," Coffee acknowledged.

"Oddjob, Tank, and Chan responding," the third man relayed and looked up at Father Beck.

"Make sure we get an enhanced shot of his face for an ID," Sloan said.

How could my heartbeat be so loud?

He took a step back, determined to stay out of the way.

"Action on 137," the fourth man said, perfectly calm.

In unison, the team's eyes went to another viewer; the flat green image remained on the large screen. Beck couldn't take his eyes off the man there. The odd angle and extreme magnification suppressed the depth of field. The long length of the alley, the dumpster, trash cans, and fire escapes all crowded together in an impossible frame around the man.

He was waiting, still as a statue. In the darkness of that alley, he'd be invisible in the shadows. Then there was more. Two people were moving toward him. On the big screen, these two were different. They weren't green. They were varied shades of red, orange, and yellow and seemed to exhale great clouds of orange smoke that turned yellow and finally green again.

"We have a Code Three. What's the ETA? Give me the tactical." Sloan was a professional.

"Code Three, ETA, six minutes twenty seconds," said Coffee.

Beck didn't see who spoke, realization forcing out everything around him. His heart was thunder in his ears. He couldn't remember picking up a headset, but he noticed now that he was wearing one.

"They've stopped directly in front of him. One man, one woman. They can't see him," one of the team said in disbelief.

"The son of a bitch works for him," Beck said, not realizing he said it aloud.

The vampire's attack was as swift as it was savage. He took the woman from her feet like a child's doll, her neck torn and broken with one motion, and then flipped her body over to land on the slanted top of the nearby dumpster with her head at the low end. Then he began to feed while the man who had brought her stood and watched in the background.

"All units, we have a Stage Two target. Repeat Stage Two." To the team in the trailer, Coffee said, "Shit, it's been twenty-three months since the last Stage Two. Goddammit."

As an aside to Beck, Sloan said quietly, "A Stage One is a newly made vampire. Still mostly human. A Stage Two has been a vampire for a while, and massive internal changes have occurred. Most notable is that they are cold-blooded and room temperature. A Stage Three has been around for hundreds of years. Their skeletons are mostly iron by then, from all the iron in the blood they consume. Very rare."

A silence seemed to last forever as they watched the infrared heat transfer from the woman's body to the vampire. "Confirm high-speed tape is rolling." Sloan sounded sick.

"Confirmed."

"We've lost 137." The man sounded alarmed.

"What do you mean, lost?"

"Looks like a manual shutdown. 132 and 141 also down." Two monitors were blank: black, not snow.

"Action on 134. Holy shit, another Stage Two." Coffee's voice cracked, discipline lost for an instant. The image on the main viewer changed to reveal another vampire on the roof of the building overlooking the alley. His only clearly discernable trait was his long hair, drawn back into a ponytail. The rest of the detail seemed lost in the folds of flowing, baggy, jet-black clothing. He launched from the roof, four stories above, to land directly on the man watching his master feeding, crushing him into an impossible twisted shape, maintaining his balance all the while. The vampire stopped his feast at the sound and whirled into a crouch to face the newcomer. Beck was glad the image wasn't color. The woman's life's blood ran down the side of the dumpster now in a rainbow of cooling temperatures. The screen switched again to show another angle. They were faced off in attack-ready positions.

They were talking.

"What the hell is going on?" Sloan said to no one in particular.

"Code Three, ETA four minutes," Coffee said in response.

"Why was the team so far away from the site?" Beck asked Sloan after covering his mic.

"We had five sites under surveillance tonight. The team was stationed equidistant from them," Sloan quietly replied.

Then it happened.

The first vampire's head seemed to fly from its shoulders of its own volition. A gaping maw was open where its head had been an instant before. With incredible speed, the remaining vampire replaced a sword into its sheath in the folds of his clothes. With one hand, he caught the body by the front of its coat before it fell. With his free hand, he produced some kind of a flare from the folds of his clothes, like a road flare. When he ripped the top off with his teeth, it ignited, and he jammed it, flame first, into the open neck wound. Almost at once, the fire flared to near inferno. The headless body was tossed, like a bag of trash, into the open side of the dumpster in full blaze. The remaining vampire paused a moment and stared into the face of the dead woman, still laid out across the top of the dumpster. He brushed her hair from her face, lifted her gently off the dumpster, and laid her on the ground.

"Code Three, ETA, three minutes thirty seconds," Oddjob reported over the comms.

The vampire collected the head, momentarily holding it up to eye level by the hair as if talking to it before placing it in a sack he wore across his shoulder. Then, lifting the crushed body of the other man with one hand, he climbed the fire escape at an inconceivable speed, not using the stairs but vaulting from floor to floor, grasping the rails and external superstructure only.

"Can we track him?" Sloan demanded.

"No, sir, all the cams on that vector are down."

"Shit. Where's Snow with the chopper?"

"Snow, ETA four minutes," she replied over the sounds of her helicopter in the background.

A tactical display of the area replaced the green display on the primary monitor. It was a computer-generated overhead view of a map showing approximately a nine-city block area. The dumpster, alley, street names, and dozens of camera positions were clearly marked by a number. A line of a half dozen camera positions blinked in red.

"Have Snow scan the rooftops along that line. That's the direction he'll retreat. Get Oddjob in to look at the scene and his retreat ASAP. We may be able to track him the old-fashioned way with the fresh snow," Sloan said. "Get Woodson on the phone. We need the area around all these warehouses cordoned off. Shit," he said with disgust, taking off his headset.

"He won't retreat along that line," Beck found himself saying. Somehow, he'd stepped up next to Sloan.

"Why, how do you know?" Sloan asked, in a tone that wasn't a challenge but carried the urgency of a man in command who needed to know.

"Because I wouldn't," was all Beck could say.

Sloan smiled, holding eye contact. "Neither would I."

2. THE DEBRIEF

Two o'clock in the morning was an unusual hour for a meeting. The crew had turned over the crime scene to the local police after Oddjob and Beeker were finished.

Beeker, Robert Ianni, was the team's resident lab tech and forensic scientist. Beck recalled from his bio how, in his days with NYPD, he had found a pattern in a series of murders regarding lack of blood at the scenes. His superiors had said that it was likely the victims were murdered elsewhere, and he had adamantly disagreed. His protests brought him to the attention of Sloan and his team.

It took Beeker less than thirty minutes at the scene. There was no need to investigate further. The entire event was on video. The hooker's murder was placed on the shoulders of the man the other vampire had killed. He was identified as the last man seen with her and fit the description of the man seen at several other "Dumpster Murders," as they'd come to be called. The local police were happy to learn this because they were to be given credit for solving the series of cruel murders.

Control (as they called the Entenmann's truck) was moved back to base. This was in a massive warehouse near the docks. This warehouse had no windows and contained seven large semi-tractor trailers parked side by side in a row, several conventional cars and trucks, two taxis, two patrol cars, and nine expensive-looking mobile homes. All this took up a small fraction of the warehouse that was used to store new wine bottles. Thousands of cases stacked on pallets were piled to the ceiling and now covered with dust and cobwebs. The import company had gone bankrupt, and Sloan had purchased the warehouse cheap.

Sloan pointed out one of the RVs as Beck's and asked him as politely as he could to change out of the collar, implying that it might make some of the team nervous.

Beck found the motor home completely outfitted, right down to cold beer in the fridge. The closets had clothes and an oversized leather jacket in the correct sizes. He changed out of his collar into a plain black cotton turtleneck. He was still trying to get used to the huge Desert Eagle .50's weight in the shoulder holster that Sloan had issued him from the armory in Control. The entire crew carried them, he was informed. The reports indicated that the Israeli-made handgun was effective against some vampires, Stage Ones anyway.

"At risk of repeating myself, Stage One vampires were recent humans. Turned less than twenty-five years ago. Stage Two's have completely transformed internally. Their digestive, circulatory, and lymph systems are all different. Past that is a Stage Three. Very tough to stop." Sloan explained.

The team indeed had powerful friends in the government. The budget for this volume of equipment was immense.

A large conference table was set up in the center of the warehouse. A single light hung above the table from an extremely high ceiling. This is where the debriefing was to take place at 0200.

The hours proved Beck had been right. Oddjob—Jim Whitecloud, that is—tracked the vampire from the scene to discover several disturbing pieces of information that he detailed in the debriefing.

"One, he was definitely a Stage Three vampire, only the second ever cataloged." A freeze-frame of the vampire's face was on a giant rear projection screen behind Oddjob. It had been computer-enhanced by Brick, the team's resident super-geek, to a very high-definition image despite the extreme magnification. He continued, "Two, this was a bad-assed mother fucker. He'd jumped from the roof of a four-story building, landing on his feet—bare feet, mind you—dropped a Stage Two and retreated in less than a minute, carrying a hundred and eighty-pound body." The video was replayed for the team members who hadn't seen it yet. "Three, the estimated body weight was 545 pounds, not including the man he carried. We found footprints in areas along his retreat that allowed impression testing and, based on the approximate size from the tapes, put him at 200 to 450 years old. Four, the dead man's body had been found, drained, eight blocks away on the roof of a parking garage. We figure he drove away from that point—no witnesses. Five, several cams had been manually shut down, and one was missing. Signs indicated it was him. This has some implications we will need to consider. Six, the remains of the Stage Two vampire were so completely consumed that Beeker, at the lab, was not convinced one had ever been there. This has potential weapons design considerations Gram is already weighing."

Diana Aubrey, also known as Gram, stood at that point as Oddjob sat down. Gram had a story so tragic Beck would never ask her about it. Her husband and two children were killed by a lone vampire in front of her eyes when she was home on leave. She was enlisted in the Army as a Unit Armorer supporting two hundred soldiers, training them in proper care and maintenance of various weapons.

She nodded to Coffee, who controlled the images on the large screen at the computer console. "The Stage Three dispatched the other vampire with a technique used in a discipline known as Iaido." The screen rolled the scene in super slow motion, clearly showing the Stage Three drawing the sword and severing the other's head in a single lightning motion. The frame froze and tracked in on the sword he'd used. "The sword is a Japanese-style katana. To date, we've never encountered any influence from the Orient. Our data shows that it is a European phenomenon, with vampires not using weapons, relying instead on their augmented physicality. The fact that he was barefoot supports the theory of oriental influence." The image returned to the vampire's face.

"The man is clearly of European, even Nordic descent, and being a Stage Three vampire, is likely from Europe. Five feet eleven inches tall, five hundred forty-five pounds, based on computer estimates. He may have the highest marrow iron density we've encountered to date. His skeleton is dense enough to set off airport metal detectors in New Jersey." Beck smiled at the deadpan humor. "He'll be very tough to stop. Although Desert Eagles may not be effective, the Benelli M4 12-gauge, with explosive slugs, and an eyeshot at that, may be necessary." Concluding, she sat slowly. The information caused a few team members to shift in their seats as they considered it.

Sloan stood and began to pace as he spoke, "The five potential sites we had selected paid off tonight. The research over the last few months and the surveillance recordings of this event will help us extensively. In addition, the man killed at the scene may shake out some more leads through known associates and personal effects at his home. Beeker, after the debriefing, take Oddjob and Shack to his apartment and do a full forensic. Coffee, retrieve the cams for servicing at first light. Book, see if we can get an ID on either of Brick's enhanced shots. I would love to get a name on either of them." He paused then and stopped pacing as if to gather his thoughts.

"The good news is no team casualties. We worked for five months to zero in on the Stage Two tonight only to have him offed for us right before our eyes, but there were no casualties." Several people looked at Beck, the replacement for the last casualty.

No casualties but the unfortunate woman and the other guy, Beck thought.

"The bad news is if we hadn't been in place, we'd never have known. A Stage Three vampire is a whole other ball game. Worst of all, he likely knew we were there." Sloan let that sink in.

"Everyone stays alert tonight. We don't have a fucking clue what happened out there. My early assessment would be a territorial dispute or a disagreement between two vampires over the amount of publicity the Dumpster Murders were getting. Famous is good for Hollywood but bad for vampires."

At that point, he stepped back and gestured to Beck. "As you have heard, I would like to introduce Timothy Beck, who, as you all know, will be joining the team. So, you must forgive us, Tim, but it will be a long night. You'll get a chance to meet everyone later, so let's get started."

Tank, Book, Gram, and Chan came up and shook Beck's hand on their way out. In the trailer, he'd been introduced to Shack, Brick, and Coffee. He'd already read the official dossiers of the entire team. The mystery remaining was how they'd all gotten their nicknames.

Everyone scattered to their assigned tasks.

Too wired to sleep, not adjusted to east coast time, and just now realizing that he hadn't had dinner, he offered the comm crew, as they were called, to make a deli run. This earned him a few slaps on the back for the thought, but no takers.

"Look, it's been a long day for you. Why don't you get some rest and we will start tomorrow afternoon with the orientation. If you want to go out and get some food, here are the keys to one of the taxi cabs." Sloan tossed him some keys. "Oh, shit. You'd better take this." He took a wallet from a drawer on the console. It contained a few hundred dollars in cash, some credit cards with his name already on them, and a badge and a DEA ID card with his picture and signature. "Don't leave home without it." Sloan opened his coat, showing his Desert Eagle.

3. THE DINER

The cab looked standard on the outside, dents and all, but had additional communication equipment like all the vehicles, including the RVs. Beck knew he'd get a new smartphone like the rest of the crew tomorrow during his orientation. He smiled to himself, thinking how they vibrated instead of ringing. It suddenly seemed so absurd. After all, he was a priest with a cannon under his coat. The bishop had given him this speech not six months ago about the new warrior-priests like the Knights Templar of medieval times. Father Beck didn't care about the speech. He'd have left the priesthood to hunt these "Things" anyway after discovering they existed. What else could he do?

Pulling out of the automatic doors, he saw Oddjob on guard outside the warehouse. All these people had their reasons, he thought to himself. Then, his mind returned to his stomach. Following the simple directions given to him by Brick, he made a beeline for the nearest food outpost. He pulled up in front of the 24-hour Stan's "Classic" Diner. The word "Classic" on the sign was probably the only new thing in the diner since it was built in the 40s.

His mouth was watering at the thoughts of overdone meatloaf and mashed potatoes. Then, before he'd even sat down in the booth across from the center of the stool-lined counter, the overweight, over-cheerful waitress held up a pot of coffee and asked the classic one-word, "Coffee?"

"Please," he said, smiling. He sat in a booth, facing the door, thinking of Coffee, the communications tech. He'd started to take his coat off but changed his mind, feeling the weight of the metal beneath, settling on just unzipping it.

There were surprisingly about half a dozen people in the diner. People came and went. Mostly longshoremen, probably fresh off the graveyard shift. Some looked like late-night club people, sobering up with chicken and waffles before heading home.

As the waitress brought around coffee refills, three more came in. They were punk types with leather trench coats and apparently too much money. As they sat down on stools at the counter, Beck thought they looked like they'd had a worse night than he had. They had pale skin and bags under their eyes. One even wore sunglasses at night.

The meatloaf was ready in a mere minute, and he dug in with a single-mindedness that was almost his death.

He hadn't heard the door open or anyone else entering the diner, but suddenly he noticed a man in a Dodgers jacket, t-shirt, and a ponytail sitting with him in his booth. The vampire stared directly into his eyes, freezing him solid.

"Are you armed?" the vampire spoke in a deep whisper, but his voice seemed clear inside Beck's head. Beck nodded, still unable to move.

"I'm sorry, Father. Tonight, this is my fault. Be ready." There was a profound sadness in the vampire's voice. Emotion flowed from it like a breeze. It tugged at Beck's heart.

How had he known I was a priest? Did I speak it out loud?

It began all at once. The punk in the sunglasses was standing at the booth with a gun already in hand. "Well, well, well. What have we here?" he asked Beck, his voice dripping with venom.

The vampire didn't wait, backhanding the man, shattering his sunglasses, and sending him over the diner counter to land unhappily among the French fries on top of the deep frier.

All three of them are vampires. All FOUR!

The other two punks opened fire on the vampire as he stood.

Someone returned fire from behind Beck with a shotgun. Beck felt the heat and concussion from the blasts, first taking one punk in the chest and then the other in the head, dropping him. But the others continued to fire into the Stage Three as he advanced to crush the nearest head with a hammer blow of his fist, crushing his skull down to the bottoms of his eye sockets. Still in shock, Beck went for his gun, realizing he was in a firefight in the same room with not one but four vampires. The first punk that had been knocked over the counter was on his feet only to find the laser sight from Beck's Desert Eagle in the center of his forehead.

Beck fired.

At the first sign of trouble, the waitress and all the other patrons had hit the floor or fled the diner. The echo of the gunshots died away. There was blood everywhere. The vampire stood by the door, looking past Beck.

"Freeze!" came from behind Beck.

The vampire turned and began to walk out slowly. He took two slugs in the back as he went out, not slowing him down at all. Beck turned to see a woman advancing with a very short-barreled, still-smoking shotgun with a pistol grip. Uncontrolled fear and panic filled her eyes.

"Stay away from the blood!" At almost the same instant, Beck and the woman screamed to the people emerging from beneath their tables. It was everywhere.

They looked at each other as they lowered their guns. Then, with shaking hands, they each took out their badges. She looked like she hadn't slept in weeks. He felt like he hadn't. She was about five foot seven inches tall and had loose blond hair that needed combing. She would look younger if not for the deep line between her eyebrows and the bags under her eyes. Finally, she lowered her head and collapsed to sit in a vacant booth. She unclipped the sling for the short shotgun and laid it on the table. Her large pea-coat, dark turtleneck, and jeans were perfect to conceal it.

"I'm not insane, am I?" she said, barely audible.

"No," was all he said. But then, he thought, *How am I going to explain this?*

***

The first unit on the scene was an NYPD rookie cop and his partner. Coffee had been monitoring the police frequencies, and six crew members were there in less than three minutes, including Sloan. He immediately took control of the scene under the banner of the DEA. All the witnesses and employees had fled already.

"Not enough action tonight already, Beck?" Sloan said as he entered. It was a question and a joke—dark humor.

"He was here. He spoke to me," was all he could choke out past the lump in his throat.

"Who?" Sloan asked, now completely serious.

"The Stage Three. Ponytail." Beck could hardly say it, looking over his shoulder at the female cop who had saved his life.

"Oddjob!" Sloan called out. "Headset." He held out his hand, and instantly, a communication headset was placed there. Sloan put it on Beck's head and activated it. Then, into his own headset, he ordered. "Coffee, record." None but the team were in the diner now. NYPD was outside securing the site.

"Already rolling," Beck heard Coffee's reply.

"Beck, report," Sloan said. It was a direct command. Sloan was eight inches from his nose.

"I came straight here from the base," he began. "I wasn't even here ten minutes." Beck looked down, and his coffee was still steaming. "I started to eat, and he was here. I never even saw him come in."

"Are you sure it was the same guy?" Sloan interjected.

"Yes, it was the same one. The same ponytail. Dressed differently, though. He sat in the same booth with me. He spoke to me. It was like he'd come to warn me. It was like he knew me." Beck gestured to the bodies. "He knew them too. These three. They obviously didn't know who he was. I also think he knew her." He paused, remembering the sorrowful sound of his voice.

"Continue." It was another order.

"This one came up to the table." Beck indicated the punk's body behind the counter. "His gun was already in hand, and he was going to kill me. He's a Stage One. I'm sure of it. I'd be dead if the Stage Three hadn't been here." Beck looked over his shoulder again at the woman. "Then all hell broke loose. She opened up on the other two, hitting both, taking out one. The other emptied his Glock into the Stage Three before getting his skull crushed for his trouble."

"Sir." It was Coffee from the base. "We have a positive ID on the woman. Her name is Maris Hodge. She's a detective from Newark, currently on suspension for shooting an unarmed man."

"She knows. You can see it in her eyes," Beck added.

"What, *exactly*, did he say to you?" Sloan asked.

"Something like, 'I'm sorry, Father. Tonight, this is all my fault.' He asked if I had a gun and told me to be ready. That's when the shit hit the fan."

"We need to get these bodies back to the lab ASAP. Police Chief Woodson won't be happy about this. Get her—" he pointed at Hodge—"back to base. We'll debrief her tomorrow." They looked over at her. She was fast asleep with her head down, on the table, in the last booth.

"Sir, I found this on the back seat of Beck's cab." Oddjob held up a sword in a gloved hand with two fingers—the sword, the katana.

4. THE LOOSE CANNON

After Beck had slept for a few hours, he'd been "jacked in," as Coffee had called it, and given the full battery of equipment. This included half a dozen guns of different kinds with ammunition, communications equipment, portable cellular PC directly interfaced with the central computer net in "Comms" (he couldn't stop thinking these nicknames were getting out of hand), night vision equipment, binoculars, video equipment, holsters, slings, ropes, knives—the pile was quite large before they were done—Christmas morning for a merc. Beck only carried the required equipment, the smartphone, Desert Eagle handgun, a multi-tool, wallet, badge, and an LED flashlight.

He was to fill the position of the deceased man, known as Switch, real name Daniel Rawn. "Loose Cannon," they casually called the position. Switch was also a former priest. He seemed to be living up to those expectations already. His primary function was to operate independently and uncover leads to be followed up by the team. Beck had stepped off the plane less than 24 hours ago, and the crew had more research to do than ever. The team seemed to consider the position to be outside the chain of command from the briefing notes. When Beck had asked early on why an existing member wasn't promoted to the slot, he realized it was not a team position, and this was a well-tuned team where every member knew his role. None wanted to change. Some couldn't if they did want to. Every team member had carved out their own role. None had been assigned.

Switch had been killed by a vampire, circumstances unknown. As "Loose Cannon," he'd been doing routine follow-up questioning in a small town outside Buffalo, New York, called Batavia. The phone logs of a known Stage Two vampire had shown several calls to a pay phone inside a small bar named Delio's. The night he'd visited the bar alone, he hadn't even asked anyone any questions. His body had been found at the local bus station behind the wheel of his truck, drained.

Three months of follow-up investigation had revealed nothing. It was just a sleepy small town pretending to be a city because it had a community college and, finally, a mall. This was precisely the wrong environment to support a vampire. A city of twenty thousand people is too small for one person a week to go missing or be murdered. Here, death was still news, not just another statistic, not just an increasing body count.

Beck remembered thinking that it would be a damn good place to hide if you were a vampire hiding from the Hunter Team.

Delio's was burned down in a suspicious fire soon after. The site was now paved to make more parking space for a pizzeria. Dead ends all around.

***

The crew took Hodge away on a gurney, and she slept that night in the infirmary trailer. Then, quietly, Dr. Franklin, nicknamed Hook (Dr. Franklinstein behind her back), extracted a blood sample from her, and she didn't even budge. The tests indicated she'd taken amphetamines for at least a week straight, but she wasn't a vampire. Hook's report stated that she was slightly malnourished, but her degree of fitness was noted as considerable.

Further investigation by the team via computers showed that the unarmed man she'd killed ten days ago was probably a Stage One vampire. His parents claimed the body and had him cremated quickly so it couldn't be exhumed for analysis. The official report noted that the parents were not surprised because he'd "fallen into the wrong crowd." An interview was scheduled.

The suspension looked like it was going to be challenging to get lifted. Her career as a police officer was over. They could presumably block any criminal prosecution for the shooting, but Newark's chief was not in the loop. Her partner refused to discuss her, saying he hadn't seen her since her suspension.

In short order, a rather extensive dossier had been compiled on Detective Maris Ella Hodge. She was single, a good detective, had a black belt, and had earned many commendations for her excellent investigative techniques. Her parents were dead, no brothers, no sisters, no mistakes, until ten days ago. Beck knew Sloan was looking at the dossier of a potential recruit.

By first light, Sloan had the bodies from the diner on ice. They'd obtained full cooperation from Police Chief Everett Woodson. Dr. Franklin would do test after test in the coming months until nothing was left of them.

Around 6:30 a.m., Oddjob found traces that someone had been on the roof of the base just a few hours ago, barefoot, without activating any of the perimeter motion detectors. In light of the night's events, the base was considered breached and had to be abandoned. One Stage Three vampire could kill them all, and they knew it. Even with all the hardware and training, they knew they could be devastated if surprised. The evacuation took less than twenty minutes, including the bug and tracer sweeps, and it only took that long because they decided to take the conference table and chairs, a luxury they'd gotten used to. Six vehicles were driven into the back of a semi marked as an Allied Van Lines moving truck. It was a cleverly concealed carrier modified to hide its purpose. All the semis had been painted for urban camouflage—bakery trucks, movers, and even a garbage truck.

Beck was responsible for taking his RV out of the city to a rendezvous point in Newark. He towed a Mazda MPV van and looked like a typical retiree touring the states. His RV even had a bumper sticker saying, "I'm spending my kid's inheritance." The semis and motor homes drove out of the city in different directions. They all remained in constant radio contact and were watched from above by Snow from the chopper. When each was sure they hadn't been followed, they went to a hangar at Newark International Airport.

The hanger had been a long-standing asset of the team. Snow's chopper could come and go from Newark with no notice. Air taxis came and went all the time with no registered flight plans. The hangar was empty except for a sizeable flatbed tractor-trailer, another RV, and a motorcycle, all belonging to Snow.

Soon, the team would be there, the conference table set up, and another briefing would begin. The pace had to slow down, Beck hoped to himself.

The hanger had been Snow's base for the chopper. It was the logical choice for the backup base. Unfortunately, once again, it was way too big for their needs. Dr. Franklin wasn't satisfied with the power hookups, but that could be fixed in short order.

Not long after arriving, somehow, Beck found the freshly awakened Maris Hodge had become his responsibility. She'd emerged from the infirmary trailer and was at his elbow before he noticed. Beck was surprised that she didn't ask any questions, offered no comments, and watched as the crew started rolling in. Everyone had assigned and well-practiced duties to perform in setting up the new base. Not moving in greased grooves yet, having just joined the team, Beck did his best to stay out of the way.

Beck felt the back of his new, high-tech wristwatch tickle him, indicating that he should put on his headset. Hodge watched Coffee unloading his portable satellite dish just outside the main hanger doors. Sloan was on the commlink when he placed it on his head.

"Tim, I want you to brief Hodge," he said. "You're familiar with the background, having just memorized chapter and verse last month, and won't be tempted to start telling stories, glorifying past missions." Almost as an afterthought, he added, "Plus, you're less likely to chase skirts."

"All of it, sir?" Beck asked. Officer Hodge could only hear Beck's side of the conversation. At that, she looked directly into his eyes as he continued, "What if she doesn't believe it?"

"She'll believe."

The commlink went silent. She was still looking directly into his eyes. Then, finally, Beck asked, "Are you hungry?" He gestured to the conference table with hot coffee and several boxes of Dunkin' Donuts that Chan had picked up earlier.

They each got coffee and a few donuts and walked to the still-open hangar doors without a word. The sun was in their faces as they settled on a stack of wooden pallets to one side as another motor home rolled in. Tank probably. The metal on the side of the hanger, combined with the blacktop, made the small spot warm and free of snow. They watched a Delta 727 take off from the opposite end of the airfield.

"Beautiful morning," Beck offered, not knowing where to start. She nodded, sipping the coffee that had to be still too hot to drink.

"How did you get involved in all this?" Hodge asked as she took a large bite of a glazed donut.

Beck knew she would ask. The version he had rehearsed in his head for weeks came out without a pause. "I was on the Pope's security detail. His Holiness treated his security staff like people, like family. He personally chose his closest dozen protectors. He knew about my past, about my time in Iraq. He knew about the things I'd been through and what I'd done. The evil I'd seen. What had… happened to me. The six I killed that night." Beck paused, sipped, and gathered himself. "When I got back from Iraq, I joined the priesthood. I was certain that Satan was taking a hand. I became a priest. I could not do otherwise. A year after that, somehow, word of my ordination found its way to the Holy Father, and he asked to see me."

"What was that like?" Hodge asked.

"He sent a Cardinal, the Vatican's Secretary of State, to visit me in a tiny parish in North Texas. He's like the second in command in the Vatican. He personally 'invited' me to come have a 'chat' with the Pope. Invited, not ordered. He left a first-class ticket. So I went."

"But how did you get here?" Hodge pressed.

"As part of the inner twelve. We were warned, but few of us believed. It explained why we carried and trained with swords and halberds over guns most of the time." Beck paused. "Then, one night while I was on duty, a priest appeared and tried to see the Holy Father in his private quarters at 3 a.m. He killed one of us before my halberd severed his spine between his shoulder blades. He didn't bleed like he should have. He didn't die like any human would have. He was paralyzed, and I didn't dare take the halberd from his back. They captured him alive. After that, His Holiness asked me to volunteer."

"It's not over, is it?" she asked. Beck was surprised to hear her voice shake. He paused, not wanting to rush her.

"No." Simple answers first, he thought.

"When this all started happening to me, I thought I was going insane. It kept getting worse and worse. The entire world was a lie." Hodge paused. "It would have been better if I had been crazy."

"The truth is always better. Not always easier, but better." Beck sipped his coffee and watched the planes come and go. So many people, so oblivious.

"How many more are there?"

"We don't know." Beck took a bite of his glazed chocolate donut.

"How long have you been doing this?" she asked.

He laughed out loud before he could stop himself. He looked at his watch. "Counting today?"

She nodded yes.

"One day." The puzzled look on her face made him continue, "I just arrived. I joined the team last night." She said nothing, so he didn't know where else to start. "My name's Tim." After licking the chocolate icing off his fingers and wiping them on his jeans, he offered a handshake.

"Call me Maris."

***

The grey Ford Taurus moved slowly through the narrow alleys on the fringe of Chinatown. The network of streets quickly became a maze the farther the car maneuvered into the district. No snow or light seemed to make it into this part of the city, only grime and rust. The strange, gritty lattice of overhead fire escapes from the buildings on either side reached out to nearly touch each other. Now and then, a makeshift bridge did connect the rusting metal stairways. Even in the winter, clothes were hanging out to dry on lines hung and pulleyed at steep angles. Some lines of clothes looked like they had been there for years, abandoned. Faded kites and windsocks hung limply, waiting patiently for a breeze. Eventually, the maze terminated in an incongruently busy cul-de-sac. A warehouse that opened into the street had all its overhead doors open, lights on, and thirty or so workers efficiently cleaned fish amid mountains of ice.

If the car's windows hadn't been up, the smell might have been too much for the driver.

If the driver had been human.

The workers waved to the familiar car as it paused for a smaller overhead door to open. The grey car slipped through just as the door was high enough into a long hallway that terminated in a large freight elevator. Then, in perfect automation, the elevator began its descent. No safety gates had closed, no buttons were pushed, and there weren't even sides to the elevator. Instead, a dull hiss of hydraulics could be heard beneath the well-tuned murmur of the Ford's V8.

The first floor it passed was a warehouse full of crates and bright lights. A forklift slid by the elevator opening, and the driver gave a formal nod as the car disappeared down another level. The next level was dark, but something moved in the shadows of that empty level. Eyes could be seen in the darkness. The next level was once again well-lit, full of men training in the ways of some martial art. They all stopped, stood at attention, and bowed when they saw the car descend. Bricks in the walls changed to granite blocks and then raw mortared stone. When the elevator finally stopped after a few more dark levels, the car pulled off to park next to seventeen other cars, trucks, and motorcycles of various makes and models, some covered with tarps, looking like ghosts in the dimly lit garage. As the driver left the car, the elevator started back up, only to stop halfway to the next floor.

The air was damp and musty. The weight of the stone above could be felt in the air.

A single bulb hung above the only door in the room. The door was dark government surplus grey with a keypad embedded above the heavy latch. The LED status light winked on, waiting for the access code to be punched. The surveillance cameras silently watched from the pipes overhead like the seven well-trained Dobermans in the shadows.

The door slid aside.

5. THE FARM

It was the strangest prison cell he'd ever been inside. It was eight feet wide by ten feet long and twelve feet high. The walls along the length of the cell were freshly painted concrete and felt three feet thick. The walls at each end were made of one-way glass. Not any ordinary glass, either. This had to be at least an inch thick and could probably stop a bullet without a scratch.

Behind the glass, at one end, was a large-screen TV with 116 channels; they were even kind enough to provide voice-activated remote control.

Whoever they were.

You wouldn't even know the TV was there when it was off. They provided a small sink and toilet at the end opposite the TV, even a shower, though the shower head was in the shadows against the ceiling. The water fell directly into a corner of the room across from the toilet on the opposite end from the TV. The water went down a drain in the polished floor.

Once a day, just before "Good Morning America," the same set of instructions would play on the TV. It was done in the bored style of a stewardess on an airliner explaining emergency procedures. A man would show how the voice-controlled TV worked, the meal/laundry exchange door, the shower, the sink, and the toilet—no explanations given as to why he'd been incarcerated, who was holding him, or where.

Every morning, the grey metal hatch in the glass wall beside the TV and opposite the elevated platform of his bed contained breakfast and clean sweatsuits if he'd put his other set in there the night before. Meals came four times a day, and the food was delicious. They seemed the perfect jailers.

Whoever they were.

There was nothing he could do. Finally, six months ago, in frustration, he screamed at the ceiling, shredded his blanket and sweat suit, and threw his food against the walls.

Nothing happened.

He went on a hunger strike for over a week.

Nothing happened.

When he placed his shredded blanket in the hatch with his shredded clothes, a fresh set replaced them. When his Tupperware dishes were placed in the hatch, a hot meal was in there at the next mealtime. Propping the hatch open all day only ensured no meals or clean clothes were delivered. Any openings on the other side of the hatch wouldn't open while this side was open.

He couldn't figure out if it would be worse to have jailers who hated and tortured you or to have them so completely indifferent. Was this a new government prison experiment, was he being held by terrorists, or had aliens kidnapped him? His mind had run all the possibilities he could imagine.

So, he got into a routine. He cleaned up his cell. His blanket and sweats were his only possessions. He had clean clothes every morning and watched TV all day. His diet was excellent. He did aerobics with TV shows after "Good Morning America" and before "Johnny Quest."

He'd examined every square inch of the cell and couldn't find a door, even in the ceiling. He'd tried to block the floor drain and flood the room, but the water was shut off before it was a quarter of an inch deep. He was sure they were watching. In a fit of rage once, he tried smashing his head on the wall and only succeeded in knocking himself out. His jailers didn't care, and they were very patient.

The days had turned into weeks and weeks into months.

He could watch whatever he wanted. CNN, HBO, ESPN, TBS, and even Netflix. The news always told him the time and what day it was. That's how he knew he'd been there eleven months, seven days so far. He never seemed to think of what life had been like before. He'd entirely rationalized that this life was better than the homeless wandering he'd suffered before. So, he resolved to wait and see what they'd in mind.

Whoever they were.

The thought never occurred to him that his jailers might be farmers.

***

"It took a long time for any organized group to acknowledge that vampires existed," Beck began. "The government didn't become officially involved until vampires crossed the path of the DEA in South America eleven years ago." Beck felt the roll begin, chapter and verse. "A wealthy drug dealer in Columbia was discovered through surveillance to be a vampire. At first, they thought he was just insane. He didn't fit the mythology of the vampire. He could walk in the sunlight, and they could see his reflection in mirrors. He had crucifixes in his own home. He just looked like a psycho drug dealer in dark shades who killed young women and drank their blood. They didn't find out the truth till they had a shootout with him that should've killed him."

Beck and Hodge were walking around the outside of the hangar as they talked. "The vampire, wearing nothing more than a Speedo, was shot more than thirty-five times and still got away." Without noticing, Beck stopped walking and talking as he remembered the photos in the file. "...But he came back. There were nine on that team, and only four survived the day. Sloan and Oddjob were on that team."

"You spend much time praying, Beck?" she asked. "Weren't you a priest a few days ago?"

He started to walk again, looking at Hodge so she knew he wasn't being impolite, but he did ignore the question. "They finally destroyed the vampire. Sloan had been wounded; they were almost out of ammunition. Oddjob had wrapped a brick of C-4 explosives in a bloody towel with a remote detonator and left it in the center of the floor in a large room. As they paused in the shadows, Oddjob saw the vampire already lifting it. The detonation almost killed everyone that was left.

"After that, what was left of the team started hunting vampires independently—listening to the wild rumors and old wives' tales. Oddly enough, the best leads came from priests in the Catholic church. They had an impressive intelligence network. Between the confessional and gossip in the parishes of the backwater areas, they turned up six more that first year. Eventually, the team convinced one superior at a time that this was a serious issue, but no funding or additional help was forthcoming until vampires were discovered in Los Angeles.

"Immediately, a secret government funding bill was passed. Sloan had resources and free rein. The Church also started sending cash, leads, and even personnel support. The Lord works in mysterious ways. The team is primarily composed of priests and former law enforcement agents, all of whom have had run-ins with vampires."

"Why don't we go to the news? Why not expose all of the sons of bitches?" It had also been the first question Beck had asked.

"Panic, disbelief, witch-hunts, innocent people being killed, mostly. Besides, who would believe? Periodically, a story gets out. Don't you read the *Globe*?

"In the last ten years, we've learned much about vampires and how to hunt them. A virus causes vampirism in the blood. It's a straightforward virus to detect, and it's a potent one. So far, once someone contracts the virus, there's no cure. It's odd to think of a cure that would result in death if successful. With the virus, a vampire lives on."

As they rounded the north side of the hanger, Beck continued, "There are several stages to the virus that take place over many years and even decades. To contract the virus, someone must ingest a large quantity of infected blood. Keeping this in mind, a vampire is usually made intentionally. An existing vampire must provide the quantity of blood."

"If it's a virus, what are its symptoms?"

"In the early stages, the symptoms of the virus are obvious. Reflexive control of the iris is completely lost in the eye. The iris wide open makes daylight very hard to take. This is believed to be a contributing factor to the myth of vampires and the sun."

Beck started counting off on his fingers. "The ability to digest typical foods disappears. The liver, pancreas, spleen, and even the secretions of the stomach walls all change. Normal food is passed undigested. A vampire also quickly loses all body fat. The new metabolism consumes it, and the new diet doesn't provide any.

"There have been cases where it, in retrospect, looks like specific individuals died of the virus with symptoms that look like AIDS. The starvation, thinness, and destruction of the immune system are all outwardly similar. These victims didn't know and would never have dreamed that drinking human blood would have sustained them. The entire system gears itself to the consumption and use of blood as nourishment. Dr. Franklin can give you all the details. She has done the major background work in the field.

"This is another reason why their existence is kept quiet. People with AIDS would all be suspected of being vampires. They've enough problems without that."

"What else?" she said.

"There are detailed files you can read, but I'll give you the CliffsNotes version of the rest.

"The vampire's skin becomes very pale and highly susceptible to ultraviolet light and sunburn, adding to the myth. The assumption is that this condition is not only from the fact that they become primarily nocturnal because of their eyes but also that, over decades, the diet lacks specific vitamins for the skin.

"After a long duration, the changes become dramatic, and the most notable change is in the circulatory systems. The lymph system assumes greater responsibility for maintaining the body's functions. The diet of blood for decades somehow changes the makeup of the bone marrow. The iron in the consumed blood begins to concentrate in the marrow. We can make age estimates by the vampire's body weight. The older the vampire, the heavier. They also become cold-blooded. It has become the primary method of spotting vampires. An infrared scan of a human shows hot core temps. A vampire is as stone-cold as the surroundings.

"There have been only two Stage Three vampire encounters by the team over the years. These vampires have lived for over two hundred years. For all practical purposes, their skeletons are now entirely made of iron. They don't bleed. They can only be killed by severing or destroying the head completely."

"Nothing like a light conversation with breakfast," she smiled. "Does a wooden stake through the heart kill them?" She was serious. "Silver bullets? Holy water? Mirrors?"

"Oddly, a stake through the heart will kill them. But only if it isn't removed for a few hours. They heal too fast," Beck explained. "Damaged lungs fill with fluid. They drown. But only if it's not removed. The other stuff is all myth. By the way, the silver bullet thing was werewolves. They are myths, too." Beck looked away for a moment before continuing. "And no. I don't pray anymore. God would not be pleased with my prayers."

***

The Jeep pulled up to a heavy steel security gate, with several cameras watching from multiple angles. The intercom responded as soon as the window was down with a simple, "Yes?"

The driver didn't say a word. He just looked into the camera as if he could see the man on the monitor.

The gate opened.

The Jeep continued along the smooth road that wound its way through the forest to the center of the 4,000-acre estate. Even though it was winter, the Catskill Mountains were still beautiful. Deer browsed in the lush clover and grasses that lined the road. The air was clean and calm.

The road finally came around the last bend to "The Lodge." It was a massive structure built of logs. To call it a cabin would be like calling a cruise ship a dingy. The outside of the structure hid that fact very well. It was originally built in the 1920s by a man who enjoyed hunting, fishing, and a lot of privacy to pursue his other interests.

The tremendous circular drive brought the Jeep to a halt just in front of a covered porch. The man went straight in unchallenged by the four guards. He hadn't seen the twenty others he knew were there. This time, anyway.

The man didn't notice the rustic beauty of the foyer or the staircase that gently curved up either side to the second and third levels as he strode straight ahead with purpose in his step. He knew where to go.

It was the main hall in the Lodge. Heads and hides of many species covered the floor and walls—lion, rhino, bear, elk, deer, and many others. A fire blazed in the massive hearth that filled one wall.

A form spoke, outlined in the inferno. "Is it done? Have your dogs found it to be good hunting?" The silhouette turned its head in profile, showing an eagle's beak of a nose.

The visitor stepped up to the hearth next to his host. "It is done but not by the dogs." The reflection of the fire filled his unblinking eyes.

"What are you saying?"

"He's back. I'm sure of it."

The host smoothed his beard, lost in concentration, his forehead deeply furrowed. The answer wasn't in the white-hot coals. After a long pause, he said, "It's been a long time. This could explain a great deal."

They stood without moving for almost an hour. The fire was no longer a blaze. Their bodies were warm now. The winter had been driven from their tissues.

Speaking very slowly, the host said, "I understand you've two new dogs." He paused before adding, "I hope they're hungry."

6. SUSPENDED

Beck and Hodge talked the rest of the morning and well into the afternoon. Hunger finally brought them back into the hangar, where it was still a hive of activity. He'd given her the rundown on the team members and told her that Sloan wanted her to join. She already knew this. Beck had no idea what her role would be and didn't want to speculate.

They found Sloan in the communications trailer with Brick and Coffee, analyzing the enhanced photos of the vampires. "Trevor, this is Maris Hodge. Maris, this is Trevor Sloan, Brick and Coffee."

Sloan got up and shook her hand. Before he could say anything, Hodge asked, "What's your nickname? Everyone around here seems to have one."

"Sir," Sloan said, deadpan. The men in the trailer lasted about eight seconds before laughing aloud at Hodge's expression. "They call me Six.

"Look, I'll tell you right now, it's not always insanity and action-adventure around here. Most of our work is research of one kind or another—system development or interviewing people who are usually crazy. Months go by without any leads. It can get very frustrating. It's also very dangerous, but I guess you know that. At least you're not alone now. As far as your duties here..." He knew she had to be wondering, "All you have to do is watch his back," Sloane said, pointing at Beck. "All hell has broken loose since he got here. And there's one bad-assed vampire out there that knows his name."

***

Beck and Hodge left the command trailer in search of food. His RV had soup and sandwich makings. The RV on the outside was a 1993 Adventure Class A motorhome. It was thirty-two feet long and felt spacious to Beck. His quarters in the Vatican had been tiny by comparison. The RV's inside had been drastically upgraded. All new appliances, new bathroom, new queen-size bed, light fixtures, cabinets and counters. A full suite of comm gear and even a 50-inch flat-screen TV. Hodge made herself comfortable in the booth, facing Beck as he made lunch.

There was another conference scheduled in three hours at 5 p.m.

Beck was stirring the soup as Hodge was reading a newspaper she'd picked up somewhere, "How the hell can you be taking this so easy? This morning, you could hardly speak. Just the idea of this whole thing had me shaken for weeks."

She lowered the paper to the tabletop where she was sitting and said, as if she played back something in her head, "I was involved with a man." Beck couldn't shake the confessional image from his head. He didn't look at her as she spoke, "I always manage to fall for the wrong guy. Anyway, I met this guy at my dojo, the martial arts studio where I train." She faltered, "Where I used to train, and he was really good. Fast, you know. The only guy I had ever met who could take one of my spinning heel kicks at full speed, in the ribs, and not budge. He always kept to himself. Polite, you know. He never really noticed me. Unlike most of the men there, even the married ones."

The soup had started to boil, and he hadn't realized till she paused. He almost burned himself.

"Anyway, so I asked him out."

"So, what happened?"

"He said no." She pushed her blond hair back off her face.

"What?" Beck let a little too much of his astonishment come through. He couldn't imagine any man turning her down. She was beautiful. She had an amazing body that made the priest in him blush.

"That's what I thought. So, I followed him," Hodge replied.

"Wait. You followed the guy because he turned you down for a date? Don't tell me you've never been turned down before. He could have been gay or something," Beck said.

"Not this guy. Besides, I had a feeling he was hiding something." She folded the paper back up. "I was turned down before by a guy that knew I was a cop. He turned out to be a drug dealer." Beck set two bowls of hot Campbell's chicken noodle on the table, with a plate of ham and cheese sandwiches.

"Well, it turned out he lived in an enormous penthouse on the upper west side of Manhattan. It probably cost five million, easy. I figured he was married, too." She continued through a mouth full of sandwich she'd just dipped into her soup. "So, I'm standing on the sidewalk looking up at the penthouse, like a tourist, and suddenly he's standing there next to me... saying... 'Would you like to come up?'"

She was blushing. She didn't seem like the kind that would blush easily. "I never made it to work the next day. I don't know what happened. For a while, I thought he'd drugged me…and seduced me. But I remember it all…" There was a long pause. "It went on forever."

She was blushing worse than before. She'd stopped eating, "I was in this giant bed when they came in." She couldn't look at Beck. "I felt like a whore. Six or seven men came in, and I didn't even try to cover myself. They stood there and talked right in front of me. They talked about blood. He was using some kind of mind control or hypnosis or something. When they left… he… started all over again."

She shook herself free of the memory and looked up at Beck. His soup was still untouched. "Dave, my partner on the force, watched my job performance drop like a rock. I told my partner it was just a new guy, but he knew it was different. I wasn't happy. I was somehow… compelled. I let it happen. I would go back to *him* every night, and he'd take me again and again. We never even talked. I barely knew his name. But I kept coming back."

"What happened?"

"I would wake up around 4 or 5 a.m. every morning with my mind in a fog, and he'd be gone. But I discovered I could shake it. I would get dressed and head home to get ready for work. One day, I met a man at the door. With my clothes on, he recognized me. He was a punk I had busted years before. The fading haze in my mind kept me from recognizing him. He followed me home. I was ten blocks from my house when he was suddenly standing in the road in front of the car. I slammed on the brakes and stopped just in time."

"Out of the car, you fucking piece of shit, cop bitch.' He held up the front of my Nissan by the bumper. The car wouldn't move. So, I shut off the car and got out. I took my Glock from my purse. My date purse, the one with the easy-access hidden pocket for my gun and badge." I could feel the compulsion in his words but let it wash over me. I shot that fucker fourteen times. It took ten shots before he went down.

"He got back up?" Beck asked, but already knew.

"I managed to get away in the car. Dave, my partner, wouldn't believe me. He said I would get fired if I told that story to anyone else. I can see why you guys carry those Desert Eagles, besides the 90's fashion vibe. So that day, I requisitioned two short-barreled, twelve-gauge shotguns. I kept one in the trunk and one in my coat. The next day, he was at the courthouse. He said, 'I'm going to kill you, and you don't even know why.' I didn't even wait till he attacked. One shot on the bridge of his nose. It ripped his head in half.

"He was unarmed. Witnesses said it was unprovoked. All he did was talk.

"So, I got suspended. I told my direct supervisor the whole story. He thought I was crazy. He may be right." Her food was forgotten. "Then, I would see them at night. It was like they were haunting me, standing on the edges of rooftops, watching. Across crowded plazas, on subway platforms. Everywhere. No one would believe me. Why would they…"

***

At 5 p.m., the team gathered around the huge conference table in the open area. Beck and Hodge were the last to be seated. The two seats were directly to the right of Sloan, who sat at the head of the table.

The katana from the day before was in the center of the table in front of Sloan.

"I will start by formally introducing Timothy Beck and Maris Hodge as our newest team members. Beck comes courtesy of the Vatican, and Hodge hails from the New Jersey

45

PD. But she'll find this morning that she has been assigned to a classified undercover operation in the NYPD Organized Crime Taskforce." Sloan tossed her a new NYPD gold shield and ID with her name and photo from her NJPD ID.

"Is this real? It feels real," she said.

"Oh, it's real," Sloan said. "It was issued to you over a month ago. "You now report directly to NYPD Police Chief Everett Woodson. And he has already assigned you to me." He slid a tablet to her around the katana on the table. "Brick, our IT guy, has already set up your email, profile, and accesses."

Looking at the files, Hodge said, "This has a signed offer letter from Woodson, dated a month ago."

"Your signature is also already on the contract," Brick said. "Plus, the NDAs, your resignation letter, all that other stuff in there you can look at later."

"You'll quickly learn that the real world is only a thin veneer. And we operate under it," Sloan said.

"OK," Hodge said. She reached up and lifted the katana for a closer look.

"Careful with that. It has quite the edge," Beck said.

Sloan continued as she examined the sword.

"This is Oddjob, Chan, Gram, Crash, Book, Shack, Coffee, and Snow. They're the Tactical team. Beeker runs the lab, and Hook is the team doctor and NS specialist."

Hodge was still looking closely at the sword when she said, "Who are Switch and Probe?"

She looked up at Sloan then.

"Where did you hear those names?"

"You guys don't talk too quiet," she said as she slowly drew the sword all the way out of the sheath.

"Switch and Probe are former members of the team."

"Dead, I presume," she stated coolly. She was looking around the table. Oddjob nodded.

"Do any of you know what this is?" Hodge asked them.

The woman called Gram answered. "It's a Japanese katana. A good one. Switch used to have one just like it."

Hodge stood holding the sword. She held it aloft so everyone could see it in the light. "Just like it? There are no other swords, just like it. This was made by a swordsmith named Masamune in the early 13th century." She paused and looked around the table.

To the doctor, whom Sloan had called Hook, she asked, "May I?"

Hook nodded.

Hodge slid a silk scarf from Franklin's neck and moved away from the table into the sunlight from the high hanger windows. Extending the katana out, she draped the silk scarf over the back edge of the katana.

"Careful, that edge is sharp," Beck repeated.

With a smooth motion, Hodge tossed the translucent scarf into the air. It began to drift down.

With a flourish that was lightning fast, Hodge spun the sword in the air so fast that most missed the motion. She froze the blade to the side.

"Are you saying this sword is the one Switch owned?" Gram asked.

Hodge shrugged. The scarf drifted down still but was now in two halves. "This sword is probably worth more than this team's equipment. Including all the vehicles and even the chopper," she said.

"Edge might be a good callsign," Oddjob said.

"That's the one the vampire left in my cab?" Beck asked.

"That was fast," Sloan said.

"What?" Beck asked.

"Oddjob picks all our nicknames. It takes a month or so," Shack said to Beck. "He just found a candidate, Edge."

"Why all the nicknames?" Hodge asked as she slid the katana back into the sheath.

Shack replied, "It's Opsec. It obscures our identities, and one-syllable, distinct names make better callsigns during ops."

"Coffee isn't one syllable," Hodge noted.

"All that skinny bastard does is drink coffee and eat donuts," Oddjob said. "Nobody liked the callsign Dunkin either."

Hodge looked at Oddjob, who looked exactly like the character from the movie "Goldfinger," even though he was an American Indian, not Asian. "What's my nickname?"

She picked up the two halves of the scarf and gave them to Dr. Hook.

Oddjob tilted his head, looking at Hodge before he spoke. "Silk? Sharp? Edge? Gimme a month."

"OK. Fun's over. Can we get on with the briefing?"

"Also, Oddjob has two syllables." Hodge sat down.

***

Hook's initial results dominated the remainder of the meeting. "The three punks killed last night were, in fact, all Stage One vampires. Book, Dan Hood, is the team's lead researcher and has dossiers started on them all. A fully known associates' workup is in progress."

"We attempted to recover the remains of the Stage Two vampire from the dumpster," Sloan said. "It was not possible."

"Some kind of Thermite device was used in that dumpster. Not only did it consume the corpse's remains, but all its flesh, and even most of its skeleton." Hook placed a small clear Ziplock evidence bag on the table. "It slagged the entire dumpster."

"And this?" Sloan held up the baggie.

"It's three fingertips. As fast as the strike to behead him was, the victim got a hand up. It was a defense wound."

"What have you learned from these?" They were fingers from the first knuckle up. Only two were in the evidence bag.

"Based on the bone's iron content buildup, this was a Stage Three vampire. Maybe a thousand years old. They do exist. Or did."

"That could explain the katana," Gram said. She was the team's chief armorer.

"Sir, there's another implication here," Dr. Hook said. "The other one on the vid may also be a Stage Three. And, weirder still, he took the head with him. The head of a Stage Three vampire would live for another hour or more."

"Look, are you done?" Beck said. "Because Hodge knows where there is another vampire. Maybe a whole nest."

"We call them Clans," Coffee said.

"Yes. I have his address," Hodge added.

***

Tank was on the roof of the building across the street from the penthouse address that Hodge had produced. Four cameras were deployed quickly, and he was gone in no time.

Chan had installed three more at street level to watch the comings and goings at the front door. It had a doorman. The infrared mode showed he was fully human.

The building shared an underground garage with three buildings on that block, and cams were installed on each level facing the elevators.

"Why do they call you Chan? You're not even Asian," Hodge asked Chan while they drove a 2016 Ford Taurus unmarked police interceptor over the bridge to Manhattan. It had a huge, aggressive push bumper in the front, dark-tinted windows, and a big chrome spotlight. Inside a big touch screen panel, flanked by riot shotguns in racks. Not very unmarked.

"My real name is Charles Weston, Charlie, Charlie Chan."

"I used to watch those movies with my dad on Sunday afternoons. That Charlie Chan wasn't Asian, either. Now I get it. Sheesh, I really should read those briefings. How did you get involved in all this?"

Chan sighed. "Yeah, you really should. I was a part of the close protection detail in the Vatican. Since the attack on the Pope in 1981, let's just say they stepped up the training. I'm an exception around here. I had no encounters before joining. Just a ton of training. So, I didn't need a dispensation from vows or laicization. When the new Pope was briefed on the reality, he felt he had to contribute more than just money." He turned the car into park near Madison Square Garden. He left it running.

"I'm going to catch some shut-eye, Hodge. Wake me up if need be. If it's more than two hours, we'll switch."

Hodge put on her headset and logged into the encrypted open-team channel chat.

> **SHACK:** Brick's got the Laser up, and Interferometry is good. There's music playing in the suite, Classical.
>
> **COFFEE:** Wagner, Tristan und Isolde, Prelude.
>
> **TANK:** How the hell did you know that?

COFFEE: I like more than just coffee.

TANK: Movement on three.

Hodge touched image number 3 in the 4x4 array of feeds on the screen in the car. There was a view through the floor-to-ceiling window wall outside the kitchen. A woman wearing a matching lace bra and panties opened the fridge, took out bread, jam, a bottle of orange juice, and then started making toast.

TANK: Human. (Visual flashed to infrared)

BECK: Why is his fridge stocked with regular food?

HODGE: Comm check. How you doin', Beck?

BECK: We are parked in an alley with the hood up.

HODGE: Chan's napping.

TANK: Now I want toast, dammit.

BECK: Did this have to be a real garbage truck? Stinks.

COFFEE: Cam 11. Target confirmed.

There was a man waiting for the elevator on the lower level of the parking garage. The thermal display indicated he was room temperature. He entered the lift and turned directly toward the camera just as it shifted back to the natural view.

"That's not him. Not the leader. Not the one… in my report." Hodge said into the headset, glad no one could see her blush.

A few minutes later, the target opened the door to the penthouse. View from one of the cams could see into the foyer.

"Face recognition tags him as Willie Goodman, born in 1991." Book said. "Minor rap sheet. I'm flagging him as Stage One, probably for at least two years to go that cool."

"Target 2 on cam 11. Same elevator. I love it when they're consistent," Coffee said as he turned and pressed the button. A freeze frame captured his face before the doors closed.

This one entered the penthouse and spoke briefly to the man in the living room, who drew a cell phone from his pocket.

Faint audio of voices became clear when the second man angrily turned off the stereo as he threw down some empty duffle bags.

"When Nick arrives, pack it up, just the essentials."

"What? Why?"

"He thinks this location might be compromised."

"I told him. He should have just killed that bitch."

The woman in the kitchen finished her toast and took her orange juice to stand in the doorway. She said nothing.

"Get dressed and get the fuck out."

Whatever she saw or heard caused her to drop the glass of juice and recoil in fear. She stumbled backward and fled to the bedroom. Brief images displayed of her gathering her clothes from the bedroom and hastily dressing.

In the living room, the men began filling the duffle with guns taken from cabinets that flanked the massive TV.

"Why would they let her go?" Hodge asked.

"She doesn't know anything," Sloan replied. "She probably thinks they're just drug dealers. And, likely, they don't feed there. Too difficult to dispose of multiple bodies each week."

Barefoot, she ran for the door, and when she opened it, Target 3 stood there. Ignoring her, he walked in and didn't bother to close the door.

This was a tall, muscled black man with a bald head and a scowl. He didn't say a word but lifted a lid on the large coffee table and drew out a hard case.

A text came to Hodge from Sloan.

SIX: Wake Chan up.

"Chan, wake up," Hodge said, and his eyes opened instantly.

"That's three Stage Ones in-house. We are going in. Tac team, GO!"

Six men in full DEA body armor piled out of a van on level one of the parking garages and piled into the elevator simultaneously. The door closed in slow motion.

"Motion on cam 3," Coffee said.

Before Sloan could say a word, all three of the Stage One vampires were without heads and toppling over.

Beck said, "That's him... the same one."

He was dressed in black jeans and a black t-shirt. He didn't pause in the room for even an instant. He moved out the front door and out of view.

"Tac Team. Warning. There's a Stage Three in the building," Sloan said.

"Comms in the elevator are out," Coffee said.

The elevator arrived, and the team poured out, firearms at ready.

"Warning. Stage Three present on site," Coffee echoed.

Room by room was cleared.

"Apartment secured," Tank announced.

"These came unassembled," Oddjob said, deadpan.

"Clearing the fire stairs," Gram said. "Up is clear. All clear up two floors of fifteen down."

***

Dr. Hook and Beeker arrived soon after. All three bodies were in body bags along with their heads. What little blood there was was quickly cleaned up.

"Sir, there's a helipad on the roof here. If you still want to stake out this place, we can evac that way," Gram reported.

"We also now have the express lockout key to level 3 of the parking garage. We can back the van up there," Oddjob recommended.

Sloan opted for the van. They were loaded and gone, and not one single witness.

"All staff, return to base," Sloan said. "Continue surveillance on this site."

"Crash, are the fire stairs clear to level one?" Gram said on the open comm channel.

"Comms may be out on the lower floors," Coffee sounded worried.

"Tank, clear that stairwell going up," Sloan ordered.

"Garage level three clear," Tank said. His comms were working fine. "Level two clear... One... Man down. Man down..."

7. HODGE'S POLICE WORK

"Six, we found Crash," Oddjob said cooly. "He's down, no pulse."

"What the fuck?" Tank said.

"Tank, report," Sloan commanded.

"Sir, he's been shot. Double tapped through his heart. Once in the head," Tank said. "Sir, these rounds went through his body armor, front and back. Plus, through the steel fire door and into the garage. There's a van parked by the door. It continued through the van and then broke the windows of four more cars before going off into the garage."

"Get out. Bring Crash. Double time," Sloan ordered.

Chan started the car. Slowly, he pulled out into the daytime traffic, saying nothing. The loading of the body bags into the van went without incident.

"What the hell just happened?" Hodge asked incredulously.

Chan didn't reply right away.

"That was him again. Same ponytail from the alley, from the diner. He went down that stairwell after dispatching the Stage-Ones," Chan said with no expression.

"Do you think Ponytail killed Crash?" she asked.

"No. Not his style," Chan replied. "This was something else."

***

Back in the hangar, the team stood around the conference table. A screen had been pulled down on the side of one of the RVs, and a projector was on the table.

Sloan came out of the medical trailer, followed by Dr. Franklin. He was carrying the tactical vest Crash had been wearing. He laid it on the conference table and sat. Everyone else then sat.

"Hook. You start," Sloan said through a clenched jaw.

"Crash is dead," she said, stating the obvious. "He was killed with highly advanced armor-piercing rounds of some kind. Not only were they Teflon-tipped, they had depleted uranium cores."

"How could you know that?" Beck interrupted her.

"If you'd be so kind as to let me fucking finish," Franklin growled. "The weapons you confiscated were loaded with the same custom rounds."

"So, they were expecting us?" Chan said. "And we missed one? The one in Hodge's report."

"Yes and no. She had a look at the three we did get, and he was not among them. He's in the wind now."

"So, you don't think Ponytail killed Crash?" Shack said as he pointed to the body armor.

"We can't say for sure. He did exit the penthouse and turn toward that stairwell." The display came to life as Brick pressed play on the video of the Stage Three taking the heads. He was out the door before the bodies were on the floor.

"That's the only stairwell on the penthouse level?" Beck asked.

"Yes." Brick brought up a schematic of the level. The penthouse took up fully half of the top floor. AC and other building services occupied the other half.

"What are you thinking, Beck?" Sloan asked.

"He was already in there. For how long? Before our cams were on or even in place. He was waiting, just like us. He hit them fast, just like we would have. He had a plan."

"It was a trap," Beck said, glancing into the distance.

"No shit, Sherlock," Tank barked. "Crash is dead."

"The trap wasn't for us." Beck looked at the freeze frame of Ponytail's face. "It was for him."

***

The silver Range Rover passed through the outer gate with no challenge this time. Through the tinted glass, he spotted several Rottweilers and Dobermans on patrol throughout the grounds.

He parked in front of the Lodge's grand stairway that led to the grand entrance. Human guards flanked the doors and closed it behind him.

Standing in the middle of the foyer was a tiny Asian woman. Her long, jet-black ponytail went down her back to mid-thigh. She wore black jeans and sneakers with an untucked white silk blouse.

"Mr. Page, welcome. Our host bids us to feast before you speak. This way, please."

Page followed her down a long hall to the last door on the right. It opened to a room that looked more like a lab than a kitchen.

"It will only be a moment."

An unconscious man was on a stainless-steel table in the middle of the room. There were restraints on his wrists, ankles, elbows, neck, and just above his knees. The woman pressed a few buttons, and tubes flowed with blood into containers. A clear fluid flowed in as fast as the red fluid pumped out.

"I've never seen the procedure before," Page said.

She handed him an elegant mug that held at least a pint. She held her own up in a toast. She drank the entire container in a single motion.

"We've advanced the harvest to a science," she said and tossed back another pint before he'd finished his first.

"I thought you only took a quart every six weeks from the members of your herd." He saw the pump stop when clear fluid emerged. About two gallons was the yield.

"We rotate stock. Plus, we need to feed the dogs. All the meat that's left will go into the grinders for the kennel. A raw diet is best, our staff says."

"Your human staff." Page finished his pint and took another.

"The Master and I are the only Clan members here. All the rest are human."

"They don't get curious?" Page finished another mug.

"One set of guards secures the outer perimeter; another secures the inner perimeter. Only one maid. She is a deaf-mute and never leaves. And after decades, it will be abandoned. Unless you can do your job."

***

Beck and Hodge were in the unmarked car going in to see NYPD Police Chief Woodson. Beck was nervous.

"I didn't think it would be happening so fast. Everyone said it was mostly boring work," he confessed. "How will I sleep tonight?"

"One can only hope," Hodge said. "About the boring part, not the sleep. Maybe Franklin can hook you up with some sleep aids."

"I will never do that." Beck wasn't sure if she was kidding, "You never know when you need to be alert in an instant."

The two of them pulled into One Police Plaza and made their way to the brass revolving doors. Hodge had her badge clipped to her belt, and Beck had his on a chain lanyard around his neck.

Beck felt like an imposter.

He wore a black turtleneck sweater, and she wore a tight black t-shirt. He didn't appreciate the "Twinsies" comment from Hodge. He wore a gray tweed sports jacket to cover his Desert Eagle. She wore a leather bomber jacket.

Beck followed her.

She looks like she knows where she's going.

She unclipped her badge and held it up for the desk sergeant before speaking.

"We're here to see Chief Woodson. He's expecting us."

"Names?" the desk sergeant asked.

Hodge just scowled.

The sergeant handed her two green V badges. "Elevator One to the top."

"Thank you, sergeant," Beck said in a tone that was so sincere it caused the man to smile. "For all you do."

They moved toward the elevator bank, and Beck said, "You should be nicer to people like that desk sergeant."

"In my experience, anyone on that desk duty was a fuck-up that's getting punished with desk duty. Especially duty that deals with the public."

"Isn't that kinda jaded?" The doors to the elevator opened. "Oh yeah. You're from Newark."

"What does that mean?"

"Nothing. I'm just tired."

They stepped out of the elevator into an outer lobby full of people milling about.

"Fuck. Media," Hodge said under her breath as she stepped out of the elevator. Like a ninja, she slipped along the crowd's edge by the wall with Beck in her wake. They passed through a cloud of hairspray and talking heads vying for positions with the best backdrop. They even slid behind the wall of people in front of the door to the inner lobby. It wasn't locked.

"Media: The other breed of vampires…" Hodge whispered with contempt to Beck.

Sliding in, they closed the door behind them. No one noticed. The entire divider was frosted glass that allowed shapes to be seen beyond but little else. "Lock that behind you, idiots, please. Not you, dear. Those public affairs idiots," said a woman behind a massive reception desk. "Are you officers Beck and Hodge?"

"Yes. Yes, we are. We're here to see Woodson," Beck said.

"Not really. You'll meet him soon enough, but it's really me you're here to see." She leaned back in her fancy receptionist chair and lit a cigarette despite the ban on smoking in all government buildings. She was sizing them up. After taking a huge drag, she leaned forward again. "I'm Betty, the Chief's secretary."

"Six said you needed an office with a direct terminal. Out of the way." She tossed an envelope on the counter. "ID badges that will get you in the garage and the staff-only freight elevators and keys to your new office." She pointed her cigarette at a private elevator behind them. "That will open on level B1. Your office," and she made little quotes in the air around the word office, "is in Long Term Record Retention. Room B11. If you take that elevator down, the hallway will go to B11."

"Thanks, Betty," Hodge said. "I like you."

"I hope they do end up calling you Silk because you'd look great in lingerie," Betty spoke her syllables with smoke. Hodge knew the comment was made to show how plugged in she was. "Still need to see Woodson?"

"Nope," Hodge replied. When she pressed the call button, the door opened immediately. "Thanks, Betty."

"Tell Six I haven't forgotten he owes me a bottle of bourbon," Betty said before the elevator door closed.

"We didn't need to see Woodson?" Beck asked her. "I thought he was Six's boss."

"We just needed somewhere outside that base to work. Slow things down. Fewer distractions. Look, Beck. We are here because this whole operation has been blown," she said as the ancient lift descended. "The night you arrived. Someone out there beat you to the target. Then again last night. You're the eleventh man. Think."

The door opened to a dim, narrow corridor that hadn't been updated since the 50s. The corridor was made narrower by a solid wall of filing cabinets. They were taking up three extra feet of the hallway. There were hundreds of cabinets—six drawers in each one. Through a gap in the cabinets, they found office B11.

The key let them in, and the wall switch lit a single bare bulb in the windowless room. To their surprise, the office had been recently cleaned and smelled of Windex. The same metal file cabinets lined this room. There was a gray metal desk in the center and three chairs.

Hodge walked behind the desk and dumped the contents of the envelope out onto the empty surface. "Here, put this on."

It was a laminated badge with his photo but no name. Just SPECIAL INVESTIGATIONS UNIT. He clipped it on his tweed pocket.

A piece of folded paper held login info. The user ID was woodson6, and the password was twelve digits and complex. Hodge didn't look at it twice. Then she slid her badge into a slot on the end of the keyboard.

"This looks like one of the Chief's IDs and access to match. We had the same terminals in Jersey," she said. She added a thumb drive to another slot and uploaded photos and fingerprints of the dead vampires.

"From both incidents?" he asked.

"Yes, and then some," she said. "How full are these drawers? I need about half a drawer."

Beck didn't ask why. He just started looking and found one a little less than half full.

"I'm going to find the freight elevator Betty mentioned and bring the car around to the garage. I'm hungry. You hungry?" Beck asked.

"Food is good. Drinks, too. And a whole box of Snickers and a box of protein bars. For the drawer," Hodge requested.

Leaving the office, Beck found the exterior freight elevator, the loading dock, and the G4 level of the garage before exiting the chief's private lift in a small hidden alcove in the main lobby. He staged a hand truck on the G4 level of the garage.

Beck got deli sandwiches and chips with bottles of Gatorade Frost that he'd seen Hodge drink at the base. He got the Snickers, protein bars, and a case of water.

His badge easily accessed the garage, and he spiraled down to the nearly empty G4 level. He parked near the elevator and retrieved the hand truck. He closed the trunk of the unmarked car, and the slam echoed in the garage.

"Father." A deep voice came from the shadows. As fast as he could, he drew the gun from its holster and aimed into the shadows toward the voice.

"Relax, Father. If I wanted you dead, you'd be dead already."

Beck couldn't breathe when he heard that voice. He could barely hear over the pounding of his heart.

"Who are you, and what do you want?" Beck asked in a shaking voice.

"Two of the most ancient questions to have plagued man through the centuries." The voice somehow had weight and had moved to another pool of shadows.

Beck lowered the gun but didn't holster it. He kept both hands on it. He was scanning the shadows all around him. When he turned back to the elevator, a large dog was sitting in the center of a pool of light. It had fur like a golden retriever but was muscled and huge.

"You have a betrayer on your team. They're giving operational information to those you're hunting. Freya will help you find them." A voice from the darkness washed over him. This truth felt like a breeze to Beck. He knew it was an unnatural influence, but it didn't matter somehow. It instantly convinced him to take the dog, and trust the dog. Beck could not do otherwise.

"Why would you help us?" Beck asked.

"We want the same thing. I thought I had rid the world of them long ago." The shadows moved. "I was wrong."

"Why did you leave the sword in my car at the diner?" Beck asked.

Suddenly, he was there, and Beck's gun was in his hands. He felt like a giant. He wore a Buffalo Bills baseball cap and a school letter jacket over a Bruce Springsteen concert t-shirt, Levi's over Nikes.

Beck was frozen in his stare.

"The katana was not mine. It belonged to Switch," he said. "This dog was to be his as well."

Beck looked down at the huge dog. He noticed the gun was back in his hand.

"Freya, *dette er ditt menneske. Gjør som han sier.*" And the dog licked Beck's empty hand.

When Beck looked up, the vampire was gone.

"Better to say nothing," whispered the shadows. "My name is Rhys Valmunin. I was born in 966. I thought I was the last…"

8. BECK AND HODGE

Beck rolled the hand truck into the small office. The dog had sat between the rows of file cabinets outside the door. Beck had never seen a dog that size so quiet. Her nails didn't even click on the floor.

"Good, I'm starving." Hodge got up, put the bags of food on the desk, and got herself a Gatorade. "Water or Gatorade?" she offered and then looked at him. "What's wrong?" She paused. "I just checked in with the team a few minutes ago."

Beck took off his headset and switched it off. Hodge did as well.

"He was here. Just now," Beck said quietly. "He says there's a leak on the team. He implied... that the leak was a vampire."

"I already figured the team had a leak. Too many written reports to not have one." She was still opening the bags and setting out thick deli sandwiches. "What else did he say?"

"He gave me a dog," Beck said and sat. "His name is Rhys Valmunin."

"Odd name for a dog," she said through a thick bite of ham and Swiss.

"No. The dog's name is Freya," Beck said, grabbing half a sandwich. "Come here, girl."

The dog entered the office silently and sat down. Sitting, she was almost as tall as Hodge sitting.

Beck held out the half sandwich. Freya didn't so much as sniff it. She raised her chin, eyes forward.

"It's OK, Freya." She gently turned her head sideways at those words and took the sandwich expertly, avoiding Beck's hand.

"That's the biggest dog I've ever seen. What is it? Part Rottweiler, part Mastiff?" she said.

"I think she's had a lot of training." Freya turned toward the door and lay down but remained alert. "I think she will spot vampires. How am I going to explain this to Sloan?"

"Why would you just take and trust a dog that's big enough to kill and eat you?" Hodge thought a second. "Why do you have to explain anything? That's what the eleventh man is. A wildcard. A loose cannon. It's worked so far," she said.

Beck mechanically ate his lunch as Hodge finished her research. "I felt compelled to trust the dog…"

After another hour, Hodge sat back. "I wish I had a printer."

"Betty could probably hook you up. Want me to call her?" Beck asked.

"Not now." She was already making notes with a stubby pencil in the small black notebook. "All six of the dead ones were known associates. All with records. Until about 18 months ago. One even had a missing person's report filed on him. Drugs, violence, looks like they were mutts for a crime boss named Evan Hawkins."

"And what of Hawkins?"

"Found in the river 18 months ago. Throat slashed," Hodge added, putting her headset back on.

Beck put his on, too, and stood.

Freya stood as well.

"I don't know how I'm going to explain this," Beck said as they headed to the freight elevator.

"Just don't. You'll see."

***

The door slid open for Valmunin. He silently stepped inside, and it closed behind him just as quietly. The space he entered was incongruent with the brutal stained concrete of the warehouse beyond. Inside, it was craftsman-style wood and lighting. Warm hardwood floors and Persian rugs filled the space. Walls were filled with bookcases, and a 110-inch high-def TV was more like a window with its 4K scene of a field of grain in the breeze with hills and a farmhouse beyond.

The large double pocket doors were open to a spacious bedroom with a king-size bed, high ceilings, and a gas fireplace already lit.

Moving deeper into the apartment, he came to the dining table, on which was set a silver tray holding two decanters of dark fluid. Without sitting, he drank the first pitcher as fast as it would pour into his mouth. The entire gallon was gone in seconds. The second decanter was emptied by half in the same manner. He closed his eyes and breathed in the scent of the remaining fluid. He finished it.

He wiped his mouth with a dark red linen napkin as the double pocket doors opened behind him. A beautiful, middle-aged Asian woman in a loose silk kimono bowed to him but said nothing.

The room she'd come from had a series of wooden pegs on one wall. They were empty except for a tiny pair of jeans and a t-shirt.

The room's far end had a platform with three large, steaming, redwood hot tubs.

She began to undress him with practiced ease. He sat on a modest redwood stool, and she removed his shoes, socks, and t-shirt. She removed his pants when he stood, never seeming to notice his nakedness.

As she hung up his clothes, he climbed the steps to the platform surrounding the tubs. Valmunin stepped down into the first tub. He stood up to his elbows in the liquid and waited for her.

She hung her kimono on a peg and stepped into the tub behind him. She was fit in her nakedness, ab muscles evident. Her body was hairless, but her short ponytail controlled black hair with white streaks that barely reached her shoulders. She tested the temperature of the oil in the tub. She tasted it.

She removed the tie that held his ponytail and took a comb nestled in her hair. She gently combed out his. When she was done, she said, "You've been shot." She rubbed a handful of oil into the angry marks on his back. "Are you injured anywhere else?"

"No."

She turned him. Standing on the bench, she was almost as tall as Valmunin at five foot eleven. She ran oiled hands over his chest to verify his statement.

"Your skin was beginning to dry. You've waited too long. If you want to pass as one of them, you must come home more often."

"I've missed you, too, Aiko." Valmunin sat, and just their heads were above the warm oil. She climbed onto his lap, and he kissed her forehead. "Please wake me in an hour." She stood as he slipped beneath the surface. She climbed up the steps hidden beneath the oil. She stood and let the oil drip from her before toweling off her perfect skin.

She was showered and wore her kimono when he emerged at 59 minutes. He stepped up and let the oil drip away for three minutes before she toweled him off, and he stepped down into the next tub.

Once again, he went completely under. Oil slicked the surface, but the skimmer removed it all before he emerged. He dripped again as she held open a black terry cloth robe.

Valmunin sat as she combed his thick hair.

"Aiko, I need you to do something essential for me," Val said, adding a series of detailed instructions in Japanese.

"Hai," was her simple response.

He walked to his bedroom and dropped his robe. "I'll sleep now. I'm warm. Join me before you go?"

***

Freya hopped in the back seat and lay down. Hodge insisted on driving.

"What do we feed a dog that big?" Hodge asked.

"I have no idea. We need to figure it out fast. I can only imagine what she's been eating." Beck said.

"There's a PetSmart on the way back to base. They'll know," Hodge said. "We should also get a collar or harness. There are leash laws. That dog is already damn conspicuous."

"You know where a PetSmart is off the top of your head? You have pets?"

"No, but I worked in Newark for fifteen years," she said. "I paid attention."

"I'm constantly lost here," Beck remarked, looking at the dog and thinking about food.

"Hey, how much does a Stage Three need to eat? Less or more than a Stage One?" she asked.

"Well, reports say about a quart a day. Less in the beginning until the body changes. Their metabolism is slower, and 1300 calories a day is enough. Maybe less if they aren't too active. Cold-blooded like a gator."

"How much blood in an adult?" she asked.

"14 to 18 pints."

"About the same as a case of beer."

"Basically, it requires one person a week," Beck said.

"Shit. Do you know how many people go missing every year? How many bodies go unidentified? Just in this 200-mile radius?" she said, her forearms flexing as she tried to crush the steering wheel. "There could be a hundred vampires right here. They could easily disappear fifty people a year. They get lots of practice. People die alone all the time. Nobody checks if they're a gallon low on blood."

At PetSmart, they got two fifty-pound bags of dog food, two big stainless steel bowls, a heavy-duty leash, and some treats that looked like beef jerky.

Their ID cards provided access to the controlled aviation areas. As they were pulling into the hangar, Beck cursed. "Shit, we need a story."

"Just say it's my dog. These people don't know me yet. Besides, it's obvious Freya loves me best," she said as she parked in front of her classic 90s Winnebago.

"Hey! She loves me best!" Beck said and got a surprise face lick. "See?"

They climbed out, and she said, "Freya, let's walk the perimeter."

She sat for the leash to be attached and heeled perfectly as they left the hangar to the right.

Beck filled the first bowl with water and set it down, then opened one of the bags of dog food and scooped the second bowl directly into it.

Chan walked over to Beck and activated his headset, then announced, "5 p.m. status briefing. Oddjob is bringing KFC."

"Excellent. I can't remember when I last had KFC," Beck replied off comms.

Fifteen minutes later, Hodge returned with Freya still on the leash. She sat when Hodge joined Chan and Beck.

"Can I pet him?" Chan asked.

"Her," she corrected. "Just don't get between her and dinner."

After the leash had been unsnapped, Freya walked up to the bowls and waited, looking at Hodge and Beck.

Beck nodded, and she lapped the water furiously. Chan risked petting her as she ate.

"Her name's Freya," Hodge said. The dog looked up at the mention of her name. "Have a look around, girl."

Freya began sniffing all around the hangar.

"How long have you had her?" Chan asked, genuinely interested.

"She was my dad's dog. He was a beat cop in Newark. A dog fighting ring there was broken up. He couldn't bear to let them put her down, so he took her home and trained her. When he retired soon after, it became his main hobby." Hodge sighed. "I wish he'd quit smoking. After he passed away, my mom just couldn't keep her. She spent a lot of time at her sister's in Florida. She was a cat person. She's gone now, too."

Beck was amazed at how easy and convincing the lies came out of her mouth. It was all true about her parents. He'd read her dossier—all true, but the dog.

After a few laps around the inside of the hangar, she was sitting in front of the hospital trailer. Beeker almost got bowled over by Freya when he opened the door.

"Sorry, Beeker. That's Freya. Sorry." Hodge and Beck rushed in to find Freya still and pointing with one paw raised. Behind the glass partition were the three Stage One vampires on stainless steel tables. Dr. Franklin was at the far end, bent over with her eyes focused on a stereo microscope.

"Come on, Freya. Good girl," Beck said, with knowing eye contact with Hodge, and the dog relaxed and followed them out.

To his surprise, the dog didn't panic when the executive helicopter appeared at the mouth of the hangar. Just a half dozen feet from the ground, it hovered and turned as though it meant to fly into the hangar in reverse. Instead, the landing gear deployed, and it gently set down. The engine shut down, and the rotors slowed, but not before it backed inside the hangar.

Must have electric taxi drives.

As soon as it was inside, the hangar doors began to close.

Snow dropped down from the pilot seat and began some kind of inspection of the beautiful craft. That done, Snow approached them, where they stood in a small circle around Freya. "Can I pet her?"

Freya looked up with the same question on her face. Snow knelt before the dog, and when Beck nodded approval, Freya knocked Snow over with face licks.

She didn't, couldn't, defend herself.

Amid this, the door to the command trailer opened, and Oddjob descended the steps and paused, making eye contact with the dog. Freya abandoned Snow and skidded to a stop in front of Oddjob. She sat at perfect attention, looking up at him. Oddjob tilted his head, looking at Freya, who mirrored the gesture.

He slowly held his hand out to pet the dog but only came 95% of the way to her head and hovered there. Freya reached her face up to his palm.

"She likes men, the hussy," Hodge said as she gave Snow a hand up. "Nice chopper, Snow."

Oddjob produced a tennis ball from a pocket and tossed it across the hangar like he was expecting a dog. Instead of chasing it, Freya looked at Beck.

"Go get it," Beck said conversationally. And then Freya was off.

Hodge and Snow walked to the conference table and selected chairs.

"How did you get involved in this shit show?" Hodge asked as they watched Oddjob and the dog.

"My story is a bit different," said Snow. "I was finishing up my master's degree in history with a last semester in France. I was staying in a beautiful chateau that had been occupied continuously since the 1600s. It had an amazing library." Snow was staring off into the distance. "I found a book that was a handwritten journal of a man named Antoine Louis, an 18th-century French surgeon and physiologist. He was originally trained in medicine by his father, a surgeon-major at a local military hospital." Snow turned back to Hodge. "As a young man, he moved to Paris, and in 1750 he was appointed professor of physiology, a position he held for 40 years. When the French Revolution began, he recommended using the guillotine." Snow seemed to falter.

"Go on," Hodge encouraged.

"The private journal said that the reason wasn't to be more humane when using capital punishment. It was because the aristocracy was rampant with vampires. It was the only way to be sure." Snow paused. "The sacks on the heads weren't to protect the victims. They were to keep the people from seeing the heads still live for an hour or two. It was all in the journal."

"What happened?" Hodge asked.

"I tried to tell people. No one believed me," Snow said. "It was bad when I got back. I almost didn't graduate."

"How did you come to be a pilot?"

"Well, it turns out that jobs down at the history factory are hard to find. After all that, I discovered that I wanted to help people. I joined the Coast Guard and became a pilot. Search and rescue."

"How did that turn into this?"

"I met Switch. Sloan pulled strings, and I dropped the team off at a decommissioned oil rig. I was to stay on the pad, ready to dust off, engines spun up and ready." Snow swallowed hard.

"A half dozen vampires all got to the landing pad at once. It was the eyes, just as Antoine Louis had described them. I did it without thinking—the reverse of safety training. I did the thing they train you never to do. I dipped the rotors and took off their heads and shoulders. One of them was a Stage Two. Sloan offered me a job even though he had to pay for the damaged rotors."

"What did Switch say when he got back?"

"Switch opened my door on the chopper and had this WTF look on his face. All I said was, 'Oops.' Switch laughed his ass off. It took me forever to avoid Oops as my callsign. After Switch was killed, it wasn't so funny. That's how we got to obtain the oil rig."

9. VALMUNIN AWAITS

Valmunin awoke alone.

He dressed in hakama pants only. Barefoot and bare-chested, he slipped out of his apartment. All the lights were on in the garage outside his secure door. He moved like a ghost behind the various vehicles to ladder rungs embedded in the wall.

He emerged in the shadows on the next level. The lights that hung from the ceiling left pools of light in the room that didn't connect.

Ten rows of ten people were practicing forms with staff. The wooden rods were various lengths, but all moved so fast they seemed invisible.

The instructor stood on a raised dais, calling out commands in Japanese. Valmunin advanced behind him like he was invisible.

He struck.

The master was bound up and tangled with both arms pinned and his feet off the ground.

The class froze and took fighting stances.

The master was struggling in front of his students. His own staff was being used against him. He was unable to breathe.

Valmunin dropped from the stage and, still carrying the master instructor, moved to the center of the room. Standing in the center of a pool of light, he dropped the man to the floor, staff and all.

The master tucked and rolled, coming smoothly to his feet, shaking his head to recover from his daze.

Valmunin stood tall, weaponless, muscles bulging, eyes glowing a frightening yellow.

With the master's first breath, he ordered, "Kōgeki!"

The circle closed and attacked.

Not one blow found its target. Bodies crashed into each other with comic intensity and minor injuries. Valmunin was moving through the room at will. Faces were being slapped with brutal force enough to humble but not harm. It was the kill shot in this exercise. The slapped attackers fell to become obstacles for the remaining attackers.

With only about ten left, they were backing him into a corner. It would be a good strategy if he were an ordinary adversary.

In the shadows, he felt the staff land hard on his neck from behind. An edged weapon, expertly used, might have killed him.

The remaining seven standing all froze.

Valmunin slowly turned and backed into the light. The staff holder never lifted it from his neck, and it now rested on his collarbone as she emerged into the light.

It was a woman.

She had blond hair in a tight French braid and a snake tattoo on her neck that had the snake's tongue licking her ear lobe.

The class all got to their feet and bowed when Valmunin bowed to her. When the bow was completed, applause began.

Valmunin joined in the applause.

She watched his eyes fade from red to yellow and then return to normal. And then he smiled.

The woman withdrew her staff and bowed to him formally.

"Come," was the only word he said to her.

As they moved through the crowd, Valmunin and the woman in his wake paused by the Sensei. Valmunin laid his hand on his shoulder and said, "Well done, my old friend." All could hear his words, and pride swelled in them all. They proceeded to the door, pausing just before the exit to bow to the dojo.

In the hall, just outside the dojo, he said, "I'm Rhys Valmunin. You may call me Rhys or Val if you like."

"Oh, thank God," she said, "it's pronounced Reese, not Rice."

He chuckled as they turned into a brightly lit white hallway. "What may I call you?"

"I'm Pamela Sikes. My friends call me Sikes, so that's what you call me. Sikes." She was nervous.

"OK, Sikes. You can relax. We're just going to the clinic. I presume you know the procedure. What do you do around here?"

"I'm a driver. I do the deliveries, get ice, the docks, random runs," she said, too fast.

"How long have you been here?" Val asked.

"It will be two years in December."

"Then you're no stranger to the clinic." He paused and surprised her with a gentle hug. "Thank you," he whispered in her ear. She felt the gratitude flow with his words.

They entered the clinic. It was bright white and sterile smelling. A middle-aged Asian man was there smiling but saying nothing.

"Hey, Doc," Sikes said to him, and he bowed his head to her in a casual greeting. She sat in the exam chair as he handed her a rubber ball.

"You know, I didn't believe any of it at first. I have no idea why Master Takashi chose me. I was an asshole." It sounded like a confession. "He told me how he met you long ago, how you saved him. Takashi is like the father I never had. His loyalty to you spills over onto everyone he knows."

Sikes didn't seem to notice the needle or the loosening of the rubber tourniquet. Her blood flowed into a glass graduated beaker as she spoke.

"It is Takashi and his ancestors that have saved me. It is my honor to serve this community." Valmunin closed his eyes.

The doctor busied himself to finish up. When the small Band-Aid was added to her arm, she lowered her sleeve, and Doc ceremonially handed the 500cc graduated beaker to her.

"It's so warm," she whispered to herself.

She looked up into Valmunin's eyes. "From my heart to yours. My life to yours. Freely given," she said as unspilled tears filled her eyes. She held the flask out to him. He placed his hands over hers for a moment before accepting the container.

She watched him drink her life's blood.

"Your strength added to mine. Your life to mine," Valmunin said. His voice washed over her, whispering feelings of gratitude.

"And still, I live all the more..." she replied, completing the small but meaningful ritual.

They both made a slight bow of the heads, and Valmunin handed the empty beaker to Doc.

"The first time I read those words, studied the book, I thought that was some real cult kinda bullshit." She dried her eyes with her sleeve. "But I felt them. It's not bullshit."

Valmunin was surprised by her hug. She was tall, almost six feet. He hugged her back. The familiar taste of her was still in his mouth. More familiar than she could possibly know.

An idea began to form…

***

The 5 p.m. briefing caught them all by surprise.

Sloan began, "Seven in less than one week. The boys upstairs are very pleased. I see additional funding ahead. They've already approved $44 million for Snow's oil rig. A permanent base, lab, and holding facility. Only an hour from here by chopper."

Gram stood as he spoke and started unloading a duffle bag of weapons onto the table. They were high-end firearms with suppressors, tactical lights, lasers, and expensive holographic scopes.

Gram spoke when he nodded to her. "We've confiscated a lot of weapons in the past. Even high-end rigs like these. But never with ammo like this." She scattered a box of ammunition onto the table and then activated a Geiger counter. Passing it over the rounds, it came to life.

"These are highly customized, armor-piercing, depleted uranium rounds." Gram passed the device over the loaded magazine pile with the same result.

"Do these present a proximity risk to us?" Sloan asked.

"These are what killed Crash," Gram said. "If by proximity you mean just being close to them… Not a high risk. Just don't sleep with one every night under your balls." They laughed, and Gram continued, "I will keep it all in the armory."

"What about carrying ten mags of that in a tac-vest?" Oddjob asked.

"Twenty-four hours in a tac vest would be like a single chest x-ray. Less, even," Gram said, tossing a 7.62mm round into the air.

"Here's the thing," Sloan said. "Teflon-coated, steel-core ammo will penetrate a heavy chest plate. These probably cost 1000 times more. Why?"

"These weren't there for us. They were hunting something else," Hodge said.

"Like what? Engine blocks?" Brick said.

"The armor glass in the cars and chopper won't stop these," Snow added.

"Anti-fixed asset or armored rolling assets?" Shack said. "Will the APC stop these?"

"I need to run tests," Gram said and sat down.

"Hodge, what do you have?" Sloan asked.

"The first three and these last three were known associates, likely recruited by a single Stage Two growing a new clan." Hodge stood and gestured to Brick to bring up a slide on the big screen. "There are two more of the known associates that disappeared at the same time. I speculate that there are at least two more out there. I built files on both."

"What's with the dog?" Beeker asked.

"Is that a problem?" Hodge replied.

"It's not a problem until it is," Sloan said.

"Freya, say hello to everyone," Hodge said, and Freya got up and wagged her tail. She went around the table, sniffed everyone, and got a pat. Hodge glanced at Beck.

"Coffee and I've developed an upgrade for the headsets. If they ever get out of direct range, they can now connect via Bluetooth to your cell phones and use an encrypted IP tunnel back to the command system," Brick said. Beck noticed that Coffee and Dr. Hook weren't at the table. "Stop by so I can upgrade your phones. There will be a new wake-word, Towson. It's a town in Maryland. Or a sandwich, a car, whatever. Not a common word, but it will open a channel to the command system. We will hear you but won't respond unless asked to."

"Coffee here, and test complete," came from Brick's phone on the table.

"Franklinstein is up to her elbows in dead vampires right now and will have a report in by midnight," Sloan finished. "Anything else?"

Franklinstein? Oh, he means Dr. Franklin.

Beck raised his hand and immediately felt stupid for doing so. "Sir, I've been reviewing the video of the last raid. They weren't arming up for us. I think it was him. They were expecting him. They knew he was coming. And he did. Our presence was just a coincidence. They had no idea we'd be there."

"We lost Crash in a coincidence?" Sloan was clearly angry at the implication.

"Hear me out," Beck said as he stood. He gestured to Brick. "Pretend we weren't there. What if the Alpha that Hodge had encountered was after Ponytail?"

Schematics of the building came up. The surveillance video played in a corner. "Alpha knew something, calls his followers, and sends them to the penthouse. What if they were bait? He takes their heads, and where does he go? Not the elevator, the fire stairs. Did he go up? No, we'd have seen him. He'd go down. Down the same stairs Crash took. Crash ran into the trap laid for Ponytail."

"But where did Ponytail go?" Sloan asked.

"I would have gone down a flight or two and crossed to the opposite end and the fire stairs there. Or maybe just chilled in a lower apartment for a few hours."

"What about security cam footage from that building?" Sloan asked, thinking he found a mistake by the team.

"There are no cams anywhere in that building," Book said. "First thing we checked. They said it's for the privacy of the tenants."

"It's a good theory. No way to prove it," Sloan added.

"That's where the depleted uranium rounds come in. What if they're required to kill Ponytail? What if he is a Stage Four, a Stage Five, or Ten?"

***

There was no additional discussion and a pile of KFC to be eaten. Several buckets disappeared with people back to their trailers or Winnebagos. Hodge and Beck sat talking with Tank.

"You're the surveillance dude around here, right?" Hodge asked as she grabbed three pieces of chicken but waved off any offer of sides.

"I like that title better than Cam Guy. And yes," Tank replied.

"How'd you end up here?" Beck asked.

"Sloan recruited me. Right out of the brig in Iraq. Same story as many here." He pointed a drumstick at Hodge. "I killed an unarmed civilian. On the same night, two of our patrol guards were killed. I witnessed one of those murders through an infrared scope in one of the vehicles. What I saw made no sense."

Beck grabbed another piece of chicken but didn't interrupt.

"It was a cold night, and we'd been having trouble with some of the diesel engines, with the combo of sand and cold temps. So, we idled some of the problem children through the night. We had so much fuel." He stopped eating. He dropped a bone. "I was trying to stay awake when I saw it on infrared. He slashed the guard's throat and was drinking his blood. The guard collapsed, and he kept drinking. I turned on the spotlight, and he stood looking at me. His mouth, chin, and chest were covered in blood. I fired. I don't even remember doing it."

"A spotlight? Let me guess," Hodge said. "You were in a tank?"

"Yep, no one believed me. Why would they?" Tank shook his head. "I had been in the brig at Al Asad for three weeks, and then Sloan was there. All he said was, "Let's go, son." And that was over four years ago."

"How does that make you cam guy?" Beck asked.

"I'm mostly a tactical ground guy. Everyone on the team has more than one specialty. Like Snow is a pilot AND a great sniper. Gram is also on the tactical team but is also an armorer. We are all on the Tac team except Franklinstein, Beeker, Coffee, and Six."

"Why is he called Six?" Beck asked.

"His call sign on his last op of his prior posting was Gold Eagle Six. He and Oddjob started this crew. Oddjob never calls him anything else but Six."

***

"Where are we going?" Sikes asked from the passenger seat of the gray Ford Taurus.

"I need your help." He looked over at her. Valmunin was dialing the intensity back, trying to tune it down. He almost managed it.

"What kind of help?" she asked.

"You aren't like the rest. You're of this age, this time. I need you to help me fit in better," he said.

"You mean the dorky Bills cap isn't working for you?" She had the casual hubris to knock it off his head by the bill.

"Yes. I think I need a haircut, for starters." He turned into

83

the early evening traffic.

"Why? The long ponytail is cool," she said.

"It has come to my attention that it is my most identifying feature." He looked at her. "I can't have that."

"You talk funny, Reese. Where are you from?" she said. "I say that right?"

"Rhys, yes. Lots of places. Norway, originally," Valmunin said. "So. Haircut first. Please."

"I think I like Val better. I'll use that, I think," Sikes decided. Val nodded but said nothing.

"Turn left, here. Then the second right and park." She pointed to a storefront with neon and graffiti that artfully said TOPS and BOTTOMS. The art was amazing. The name of the salon was boldly rendered in red and gold-like flames. It was surrounded by scenes of biker chicks on choppers, guns firing, tombstones, brick buildings with fire escapes, and musicians playing instruments or smashing guitars. Chaos and glory from a half dozen different artists.

It was a combination hair salon and tattoo parlor.

The old-fashioned bell rang as they entered. A woman was sitting in one of the four matching dentist chairs, ignoring all the TVs that seemed to be playing different horror films, some in black and white. She was focused on a smartphone. When she looked up, she recognized Sikes and squealed hellos in delight.

"And who do we have here, and can I have him when you're done with him?" she said.

"Val, this is Eve," she said with a gesture, "Eve. Be nice. He's kinda my boss. He owns the company I work for."

"Very nice to meet you, Val." She extended her hand. Valmunin took it and gave it a gentle squeeze and shake. Eve had full-arm tattoos, and the low-cut torn t-shirt allowed the tats on her full breasts to peek out. "What do you need this evening, darlin'?"

"Not me, him." Sikes motioned for him to sit.

"And what'll it be?" Eve asked as she covered him with a Batman cape. He turned to Sikes and deferred with a nod.

"I get to decide, eh?" She looked up at a collage on the wall. She plucked a rubber band off that was hanging on a push pin. "I think that one, cut and color." She pointed at a photo.

Sikes cinched the rubber band high on his ponytail and boldly cut it off near the base of his skull.

She waved it under Valmunin's face.

She's not afraid of me at all. Even knowing what I am.

"I'm keeping it," Sikes said as she stuffed it into her pocket.

An hour later, they were done there. It completely changed him. He seemed taller.

"Thank you, Eve," Val said, handing her a wad of cash, not bothering to count or even ask the price.

"You are quite welcome, darlin." Eve flirted, "Come see me any time." The bell echoed behind them.

Next, they were in an expensive leather shop where they had to pay extra for a leather jacket that was already broken in. It was a quick purchase, as Sikes was decisive.

Last, his Nike sneakers were replaced with Timberland men's black waterproof ankle boots. These met his soft sole requirement for silent movement. Upon hearing this, Sikes also made him buy a pair for her.

Sikes deemed his black jeans and Pink Floyd Dark Side of the Moon t-shirt adequate.

"Look. I gotta be honest." Sikes was walking backward in front of Valmunin on the way back to the car. "You look different, especially the dark hair. But you aren't really... inconspicuous."

She pulled the blond ponytail out of her pocket. She looked at it one more time and then stopped walking. Val stopped as well.

She offered the ponytail back to him.

"No, you keep it. You earned it and more," Val said.

"More?"

"You must be hungry," he said. "I've already had dinner."

"Wow." Her eyes were wide. "You literally just said that."

"I find humor difficult. I get to use it so infrequently," Val said.

"I know a great steak place I can't afford that's near here."

It was late, so they didn't have to wait. They were seated in a private booth that was meant to be romantic.

They ordered steaks and an expensive bottle of wine.

When the waiter was gone, Sikes asked quietly, "Look, if this is too personal, just tell me to fuck off, OK?"

Valmunin smiled, amused. "OK."

"Can you even eat regular food? Drink regular stuff?"

"I can, but rarely do. Most food has no flavor for me. A rare steak has some flavor but doesn't sustain me. I enjoy wine, but alcohol has no effect. I must be cautious with my diet."

"Are there many like you?" she asked as a cloud of sadness covered her face.

"None, like me. Until recently, I thought I was the last."

"How old are you?" Sikes asked.

Valmunin smiled. "I'll tell you if you tell me how old you are."

"I'm 29. I was never one to keep it secret."

"I was born in the old village of Akra, Norway, in 966. I'm 1049 years old."

"Are you lonely?"

This was not the question I expected.

When he didn't answer right away, she continued. "Do you ever have…companions? Or friends that…don't know?"

Valmunin sighed. "I had a companion once. We were together for just under 300 years. She was captured and burned at the stake for being a witch."

"I'm sorry. You don't have to talk about it. I'm sorry." Sikes was.

"You ever hear of a dunking stool? They'd bind you to it and hold you underwater for an hour. If you lived, you were a witch. Technically, a vampire. She wasn't strong enough for her chains. And they burned her alive."

"I'm sorry." Sikes placed her hand on his. He knew it was cold.

"Don't be. She knew she deserved it. So did I. We were monsters then. I still have her skull in my den. She reminds me of what we were."

They fell into silence when the food arrived. Valmunin ate the steak, drank wine, and even ordered dessert and coffee.

After his first sip, Val asked, "You ever have a dog?"

"We had two when I was growing up. The first one my parents had before I was born. His name was Jesse. He died when I was nine. We got Apollo after that. Mutts both. He died when I was 25. I haven't been able to afford another since. One day."

"Did you love them?" Val asked, sadness dripping from his voice somehow.

"More than anything. They were family." Sikes had a sudden realization about the question.

"And despite the pain and loss, you'd do it again?" Val asked gently.

Sikes didn't answer right away. Unselfconsciously, she wiped tears from her eyes.

"I haven't cried for years, and you do it to me twice in one evening. I get it. I get it. I'll be like your fourth dog. I'm cool with that."

He smiled. She threw her napkin at him.

10. THE PARKING GARAGE

"I quickly discovered that the best coffee around here is usually in the command trailer," Beck said as he and Hodge walked across the quiet hangar towards the Entenmann's tractor-trailer.

The hangar doors were still closed, but the dawn light streamed in from the high windows.

They walked up the steps and went in.

Sloan was on duty, as usual. It sounded like he was on a call with a logistics firm regarding guaranteed supply chain issues.

Brick and Book were both there at research workstations with multiple screens. Sloan was standing, so there were four empty seats.

Beck went to the large ornate electric coffee urn in the small galley kitchen and filled his mug. Hodge followed him.

"Where's Coffee? I didn't know you allowed him to leave his post," Beck said.

"I swear he'd never get out if he didn't require fresh coffee beans," Brick said seriously. "We make him leave at least once a week for a real shower. I swear all he eats are Pop-Tarts and Hot Pockets."

"Hodge hasn't met him yet," Beck said. "What are you looking at here?"

Brick had a map up of the Bronx. There were lots of dots with numbers floating over points on the map.

"These are reported missing persons that were also homeless." Brick zoomed out, and there was a definite cluster there. "Now, it could be that the beat cops there have a better relationship with the homeless, and reporting is just higher. Another theory is that the suicide rate is higher there, and the river is a common method and also takes the bodies out to sea. But we think someone may be taking them. And these are just the ones reported."

"Probably half of the Bronx homeless are loners that no one would notice if they went missing," Book added.

"Is there a big homeless population there? The Bronx sucks in the winter," Hodge said. "I know there is here, where all these bridges go over the railroads and highways by the hospital here. Right in the center of this cluster. Can you bring up the last 10 or 20 MP cases from in this cluster? Send them to my phone, please."

It took Brick only a few minutes. Hodge and Beck had electronic copies of the cases on their phones and were moving out.

"Let me put you on hold for a second." Sloan pressed the hold button on his console. "Do I need to have a full tactical team shadow you two today?"

Hodge replied, "Nah, just doing leg work today. You can only get so far with data crunching. It may become clear why a cluster of MPs are here. It might be because of the proximity of the hospital. Sick, homeless people might cluster there and might die unidentified in the ERs. Other reasons like that."

Beck saw Brick and Book look at each other and dove into this new line of research.

"Age info would also be handy," Hodge said over her shoulder. "And active gangs in the region. It's the fucking Bronx."

As they descended the stairs, Freya waited for them. Beck grabbed a case of water off a nearby pallet and headed for the car.

"Thirsty?" Hodge smiled.

"It's for the dog. I found an old Tupperware bowl in the back that was already in the Winnebago."

The case of water went in the trunk, and they were off. Someone else had opened a small overhead door on the side. Hodge tried the overhead door opener built into the visor, and the door began to close.

"Those techs are good," she said.

"Are they, though?" Beck asked. "Why are they even running ops in that trailer? They should be in a permanent base, hardened and secured. Because if just one Stage Two gets in there, it's over."

"Operations have growing pains. This setup is probably way better than last year and the year before," Hodge said as she drove. "Snow said that they acquired an offshore oil rig. That would be a perfect base. Three helipads, housing for like sixty people. Kitchens, labs, generators, solar, water desalinization, and best of all, privacy. They're making this shit up as they go. While trying not to get killed."

"We are hunting prey that can hunt us back," Beck said.

They rode in silence for a while. They just drove around for an hour when they reached the area in question. They saw several homeless encampments.

For the next three days, it was all the same. Tents and blue tarps, mostly. There were a few tin roof shacks and many vans with no wheels incorporated into makeshift living spaces. The areas always smelled of shit and piss and vomit.

They were beginning to think they were pulling at the wrong thread.

Graffiti covered all the surfaces beneath the bridges, and Hodge was able to decipher the gangs that operated in this area based on the tagging, it was the border between the two gangs.

They parked in a commercial, privately owned garage built adjacent to the hospital's main garage. The rates here were much lower than the hospital parking. It was mostly full, and they found a spot on the 7th floor.

Freya was excited but was trying not to sniff every damn thing. The elevator smelled of urine and fresh spray paint. It opened to a small lobby covered on every side with many layers of graffiti.

Freya was on her leash but was all business now. Every time they paused, she sat. Every time they walked, she heeled perfectly between them. They crossed the four-lane road to the opposite side when the traffic allowed.

The entrance to the homeless encampment was flanked with so many wheelless, stripped shopping carts that it made a kind of gate.

Beck quietly said to Freya, "Be nice." And her tail began to wag rapidly, and her tongue hung out in what he called her dumb happy face.

Because the bridge was so low and wide here, the ground was dry and free of mud and snow.

The camp was nearly deserted except for a girl in her late teens tending a fire in a shopping cart on its side. She was feeding pallet boards in from the end—a black charred saucepan boiled as she added a packet of ramen noodles. A kettle next to it began to whistle. The girl had an oven mitt that looked like a cow puppet.

Beck held up his badge to the girl. "My name is Timothy Beck, and I am with the Special Investigations Unit that's looking into a pattern of missing persons cases. Can we ask you a couple of questions?"

The girl didn't answer. She didn't even look up as she poured hot water from the kettle into a tall ceramic mug. She produced a well-used tea bag from her pocket and added it to the water. She set the cup aside and stirred the ramen.

"Never saw a cop come down here before. Specially with no dog. We stopped asking," the girl said. She was probably only 15 or 16 years old. She might even be pregnant. The oversized dirty parka may have been intentionally hiding it.

Hodge took a money clip from her pocket and stripped off five twenty-dollar bills.

"We'd appreciate it," Hodge said, holding out the cash.

The girl looked around and, seeing no one else, took the cash and slid it into her oven mitt.

"Do you know anything about where these people go?" Beck asked.

"Most just drift off. Go out for the day and never come back. Find a better crib, a better camp. A lot of the boys join the gangs. Sometimes we see them again. Some girls get hooked on drugs, pimps, and trafficked. Lucky ones get rescued, never seen again." She stirred her ramen like she'd said something she shouldn't have said.

"Rescued?" Hodge peeled off another twenty but didn't hand it over.

"When it gets real cold, mostly." She lifted the ramen off the makeshift grill. "Guy that runs the garage sometimes helps—got a little shed with cots, sleeping bags. I think he fucks them. Suck his filthy dick, or get the fuck out. Ain't doin it."

"How does he rescue?"

"Sneaky fucker. Finds out if you've family or not. Calls 'em. Not doin' it. What's your dog's name?"

"Freya," Hodge said gently.

"I miss my dog," the girl said.

"Can we call anyone for you?" Beck asked.

"If you go over there, don't tell Kapelos you spoke to anyone here."

Hodge produced another twenty.

***

Hodge was driving as they descended level after level. It got a lot darker when they were finally entirely below ground. Two more levels, and they finally saw the office door the girl had mentioned.

Their headlights were on as they pulled up to the front of the office. Cinder blocks had been added between the 3x3 concrete columns to build the office. A steel door with a wire mesh security window was propped open with an old cinder block that had been spray-painted yellow long ago.

They walked into the office. Two steel desks were facing the front, and a woman was sitting at one of them. She was about fifty years old and a bad blond hair color and style. "The Price is Right" was playing on a TV in the corner. When she noticed their badges, she muted the TV and stubbed out her cigarette.

The other desk was piled high with pizza boxes, just delivered by the smell.

"Can I help you?" she said nervously as she noticed the massive dog at their side sitting still, eyes slowly scanning the room.

"You must be hungry," Hodge smiled, joking.

"I don't eat that. I'm vegan." She lit another cigarette.

"We'd like to speak to Mr. Kapelos, please," Beck said politely.

"Who may I ask is calling?" she said as if they were on the phone, not standing there.

"Detectives Hodge and Beck," Hodge said, wrapping the leash tighter around her fist. Freya was sniffing furiously.

"Just a moment." She got up and went through the door in the center of the back wall. It was cheap paneling. One side of the door had a whiteboard with two weeks in a grid. Names along the left showed who worked and when. The secretary must have been named Doris because it was the only female name.

A time clock where employees punched in and out was on the other side of the door. Four employees, including Doris, were punched in.

Doris came out, closed the door behind her, and sat down before saying, "Mr. Kapelos is very busy today. He says unless you have a warrant, he won't have time for you today." She lit another cigarette. Her hands were noticeably shaking.

"Well, we don't have a warrant, but our drug-sniffing dog seems to be onto something." Without another word, Hodge moved forward and barged into the back office. Beck followed.

"Mr. Kapclos, I presume?" Hodge said as Freya froze. Her head was lowered, her nose pointed at the man, and her right front paw was raised.

"Officers, forgive me, but I can't talk to you without a lawyer present. These are very litigious days, and my lawyer would never let me hear the end of it."

He said all this from an oversized, dirty, overstuffed recliner. He was wearing a dirty white tank top. He was skinny, and his skin was papery and dry. His hair was wispy and balding. His eyes were sunken. He had a lit cigar in his mouth.

"Do you own this garage?" Beck asked, ignoring his words as his mind raced.

"As I said, lawyer or we don't converse."

"Fine with us. But as you can see, our dog here thinks we are onto something. We will just need a few minutes of your time. We had a tip that drugs were stored in Rubbermaid sheds down here, and sure enough, there are the sheds."

Kapelos thought for a minute, then made a decision.

"OK, OK, I'll get the keys. Look all you want," he said as he got up and hobbled to the front office. He opened a lockbox on the wall and took out a key ring.

To Doris, "Get Isaac on the phone and tell him to get over here." This garage level only had a few dusty cars parked on it. "Long-term parking here only."

Four of the twelve 10x10 sheds were locked. He unlocked them and opened them all.

The locked ones had two cots in each. Empty milk crates made makeshift end tables between them.

"I let employees sleep here sometimes. I don't charge rent."

Hodge detached the leash and said, "Freya, Search." The dog began to go from shed to shed, sniffing. There was a construction site-style porta-potty halfway down the row.

"Why so many sheds?" Beck asked.

Kapelos had his arms crossed and watched the dog. "Look, man, you see that homeless colony across the street? They were coming in here when the weather was super cold, windy, and they were peeing all over. So, I got a porta-potty to stop guys quitting all the time instead of cleanin' up their shit. Gotta understand it was families mostly. You know, with kids, pregnant women, and shit. The sheds I let 'em… use. When it's terrible outside." Kapelos grew quiet when he saw where Freya was sniffing.

Beck turned on a powerful flashlight and revealed a dark gray door on the corner of the office's wall. The door had two deadbolts in addition to the knob. The door was painted the same color as the wall, making it invisible in the shadows.

"For your safety, sir. I will need you to put your hands behind your back for me…." Hodge began.

Beck heard but didn't see him strike Hodge. When he wheeled around, drawing his Desert Eagle, the powerful flashlight shined directly into Kapelos's face as he began to advance.

He shot Kapelos in the crotch. He didn't mean to. But it shattered his pelvis, where it attached to his spine. Beck's second shot went wide, shattering Kapelos's humerus bone as he went down. Before Beck could aim again, Freya crashed into Kapelos with her full weight, teeth bared.

"Freya, if he moves, bite his head off like the last one," Beck said.

Kapelos was cursing under his breath. The paper-thin skin of his arms was torn but not bleeding.

Beck kept his gun sighted on Kapelos while he checked on Hodge. She was already starting to sit up.

"Six, come in," Beck said, his ears still ringing.

"No signal down here. Fuck," Hodge said as she staggered up.

"Go use their phone. We'll watch him," Beck said.

Hodge shot Kapelos again. Twice. Once in the ass, shattering his pelvis further, and in the elbow of his remaining good arm. Freya didn't even flinch.

"You fucking bitch," he cursed at her through clenched teeth.

Beck watched him as Hodge ran to the office. His dry skin had ripped at the wound sites of his arms. A clear, yellowish fluid, like honey, seeped out.

Hodge was back quickly with the car. Headlights faced Kapelos. The car's strobes were on. Doris was soon cuffed and locked in the back.

"She didn't call the cops. She had explicit orders NEVER to call the cops. Alpha team ETA is nine minutes."

"You've no idea what you're dealing with," Kapelos growled.

"Oh, I think we do know, dipshit." She shot him again in the leg.

"Jesus, warn me next time," Beck said as Hodge took manacles and chains from the trunk. Blood ran down from above her ear.

She roughly manacled his hand behind his back, his ankles together, forcing his knees to bend at a cruel angle, and hog-tied him. Only then did Freya back away, but not far.

"Who the fuck are you, people?" Kapelos demanded.

Neither of them answered.

Hodge went to the unmarked patrol car and opened the back door to where the wide-eyed Doris sat. "What's behind that door, Doris?"

"I don't know. I've never seen it opened," she sobbed.

They heard Freya begin to growl. Across the garage, they saw a man enter the office and come straight out with a fire ax from the wall. He was running directly at them. Freya was next to Beck, ready to attack. Beck was sighting in, center mass again. His flashlight illuminated the man.

"Freeze! Police!" Beck shouted.

He kept advancing.

This was the loudest shot yet. Hodge fired from behind him. The heat from the fireball felt like it scorched him.

The shot took the top of the man's head clean off. His feet flew into the air like he'd been clotheslined. This one bled.

"Stage One," Hodge stated. "How many are on this shift?"

"Three, plus Doris." Doris was on the floor of the cruiser now.

So, there they waited.

Freya on alert, Beck and Hodge waited with guns drawn for the last four minutes.

***

Three black Hummers rolled in, followed by a yellow cab, the old kind. The team in full body armor rolled out and took up a perimeter.

Oddjob and Sloan walked up as Beck and Hodge lowered their weapons.

"I can't leave you two alone for a second, can I?" Sloan looked in the back of the unmarked cruiser.

"There might be two more. They're clocked in, but I don't know where they are. Doris might be able to help."

"One will be in the exit booth. The other could be anywhere," Doris said, rushing to be helpful.

"Go," Sloan ordered Tank.

Tank pulled down a Velcro flap revealing a bright yellow "POLICE" banner on the front of his tactical vest. Then he pulled one down on Chan's back before turning so he could do the same. Tank, Chan, Gram, and Book piled into a Hummer and rolled.

Oddjob walked up to the hogtied vampire and, with considerable effort, lifted him by the bar that connected his wrists and ankles like he was luggage.

"We have us a Two," Oddjob noted his weight as he carried him over to the nearest Hummer. As the back opened, what looked like a coffin slid out, and Sloan opened it. He and Oddjob placed the man inside it, face down.

Latches were secured all around the lid, and Sloan activated some controls at the foot. "This floods the compartment with argon gas. We don't know why it makes them unconscious after a few minutes. It's odorless and colorless. They don't notice it."

"Booth's empty, sir. He rabbitted," came over the headset. "The gate has been crashed. Probably him?"

"Remove the other gate so people can come and go as they please. Then, use the Hummer to block the ramp to this level."

Hodge held up the keys and rattled them.

"Do we wait or have a look?" she asked. But then she went to the door and started trying the keys.

Oddjob distributed SCAR carbines with the tactical lights already activated. They were new to Beck. A variant of an AR15, commonly called an assault rifle.

One key fit. The steel door swung inward onto a landing above a wood staircase that descended into the dark. A dim light was on below. There was another level below this level of the garage.

Freya ran past them all and was down the flight in two leaps. She was around the corner and out of sight in one second.

Then, the screaming began.

In two-by-two formation, they rapidly descended. Rounding the corner at the bottom of the stairs, Beck realized there was a whole other level to the parking garage. The office was built over the ramp, concealing it. This level was filled with twenty-foot STEEL shipping containers in every parking space.

They moved out into the garage, following the sound of Freya's growl. It was constant, like a low rumbling thunder.

The level smelled of a strange combination of welding rods, cut steel, and urine. As they moved along the rows of shipping containers, fingers appeared in small horizontal slits at eye level and floor level.

"Help us," whispered a voice from behind the slits. "Ayúdanos…"

They kept moving.

In the center, beside the closed elevator, the container walls made a room about 40 feet by 40 feet. The area was well-lit and painted white. The floors, ceiling, pipes above, concrete pillars, walls, and even the shipping containers facing the area were all white.

It looked like a makeshift hospital. There were four hospital gurneys with I.V. trees attached. There were two stainless steel tables, cabinets, and tool chests, all on wheels.

On the floor in front of them was a severed hand, whose owner was cowering in the corner just beyond. Freya was still growling. Her hackles were up, making the giant dog seem like a werewolf of nightmares.

The cowering man held the stump of his arm tight to his chest. His eyes rapidly went from Oddjob to Freya and back, his fear growing.

Hodge walked up as she finished pulling on some heavy-duty black latex gloves. She knelt at eye level with him before she spoke.

"We can do this two ways, vampire." She stared into his face, "A tourniquet or a body bag. I don't give a fuck either way. Either way, they will be carrying you out, not me. So what'll it be?"

Without a word, he held out the bloody stump, despite the laser dots on his face. Both the ulna and radius bones showed. Hodge expertly slid on the tourniquet and tightened it down cruelly.

"Get up on the gurney." He complied without question, and Oddjob began strapping him down as Hodge and Sloan pointed Desert Eagles at his head.

Beck was examining the equipment. "They're taking blood like a blood bank or the Red Cross."

"Yes. Yes," The man on the gurney said in a thick Pakistani accent. "We don't kill. We feed them. They feed us."

"I got that. What do you tell them?" Beck held his gun up. Anger was evident on his face.

"Rich people, powerful people, in hospital need their blood. We tell them to cooperate or… take organs, too. Kapelos idea. All Kapelos idea."

"HOW MANY?" Beck yelled at him.

"Fifty-one. Only fifty-one." He cowered.

"That's what the pizzas were for. Jesus," Hodge cursed.

She went to the closest container. Eyes stared back at her from the slit cut onto the door.

"Do you understand me?" she said to the slit.

"Yes," came a small female voice.

Hodge shined her flashlight through the slit. The door had no lock, just a carabiner where a lock would normally go, so she opened the door.

Inside there were two women. They sat on flimsy aluminum cots. There was a pile of pizza boxes and a 5-gallon bucket by the door that opened. A large trash barrel lined with a large black bag was positioned to give a little privacy to use the bucket. Above those was a single shelf with a half a dozen rolls of TP and two boxes of wet wipes.

One of the girls lay down on the cot. The other stood and walked slowly up to Hodge.

"We are the police. You're safe now," Hodge said as Beck went to the girl who was lying down.

"She'll be OK in a day or two. She donated today," said the first girl. She looked back into the container at her cellmate. "It's double ration night if one of us donates that day." She was forcing cheerfulness.

"Oddjob," Beck called out. "Box that guy for transport and then bring down those fifty pizzas on a cart in Kapelos office. Take the elevator."

Oddjob discovered that there was no button for this level. A key had replaced the button. Oddjob convinced the Stage One to give up the key. It had been on a chain around his neck.

Oddjob had no idea how recent a Stage One he was. The argon managed to suffocate him within just 40 minutes.

They questioned several of the girls over pizza. They were all girls. All homeless. All had been taken from the surrounding populations. Most had first come through the 10 x 10s on the level above. Most had been promised new lives. They had even said goodbye to their friends in the homeless camp. And they'd woken up here.

They all had a roommate. The roommate was used as leverage and as a nurse to help the donor.

They all believed it was corrupt doctors helping the rich. They knew there were others. They could see through the slot to neighbors across the aisle. If they tried to talk to neighbors, they were punished. No food for days or moved to the head of the donor line. Some disappeared. They thought Kapelos raped some.

Kapelos was not what he seemed.

Chief Woodson arranged for all the girls to be safely transported to an upstate NY women's shelter. None of the freed prisoners had any idea what really happened to them. But they would now be safe.

***

Chan rode back with Beck and Hodge. He sat in the back with Freya, to her delight.

"Franklinstein is going to have a lady-boner for a month, thanks to you guys," he said. Freya licked his face, "Our first live Stage Two. Did you really shoot him in the dick? That's cold. Weren't you a priest just last week? Stone cold, man."

"I was a Swiss guard in the Vatican. A priest as well. Roles change, vows change as well," Beck said. Chan was not hearing the subtext that he didn't want to talk about it. "I'm so tired I need to sleep when we get back."

"I can cover for you if Six holds another of his debriefings," Hodge said.

"Thanks," Beck said. They rode the rest of the way back to base in silence. Freya settled down and fell asleep in Chan's lap.

The base seemed empty when they returned.

"Coffee, we're back. I'm going 10-7. Beck out."

"Roger that. Good work today, Beck. I'll make sure nobody bothers you," Coffee added.

He kept his word.

***

Beck's bladder forced him to wake to sunlight in the Winnebago. He wore gym shorts and a DEA t-shirt while he slept. All were clothes provided by the team. He sat up and yawned, trying to get his ears to pop. His feet touched his black

Velcro close sneakers, positioned where he could put them on in an instant. To his left was a ready rack with a Colt M4, a Mossberg 590 12ga, and his Desert Eagle 50cal.

He rubbed his face, knowing he needed a shave. He smelled coffee.

He stood up and saw Freya sleeping at the foot of his bed. He quietly stepped over her and into the bathroom. It took a very long time to empty his bladder. Stepping out and into the kitchenette, he poured a cup of coffee and found Hodge sitting in his booth, sipping coffee and reading a tablet on a table covered in reports.

Beck was startled and almost spilled the coffee.

"Warn a guy, will ya? Make a sound. Say good morning or something. If I knew you were here, I would have at least closed the damn door."

"That bladder would be damn handy on a long boring stakeout," she said as she sipped her coffee and sighed.

"Boring stakeout. Let's do that. I could use a bit of something boring. They promised me I'd be bored, a lot. Let's do that. What time is it?"

"It's 7:05 a.m. You slept for almost twelve hours," she said, still studying her tablet.

"You get any sleep? You look better. You look good," Beck said and then exaggerated the joy he took in his coffee sip.

"You, too. Keep the beard. It takes some of the priest off'n you," she said. "I can see now why they call her Franklinstein behind her back. Our infamous Dr. Hook has been up all night dissecting our latest captures first."

"That's her job, isn't it?" Beck asked as he tried to read the report upside down.

"Yes, but just to warn you. I figured before breakfast was better." She laid down her tablet on the table, spun it around, and slid it over to him. "We confirmed he is a Stage Two. At least 200 years old."

"You got to be fucking kidding me." The image was Kapelos strapped down on a gurney, naked, with both arms fully restrained to the shoulders and his legs at the hips.

"It turns out it is the standard containment protocol. Sloan's standing order," Hodge said.

"Jesus, I really did shoot him in the dick," he said, zooming closer at the coarse stitches all over him.

"Good luck with a nickname," Hodge said.

"The iron content in his femurs confirms his age. Plus, he's talking. He's not stupid, either. He knows he's at our mercy. As long as he talks, he's an asset."

"Lefty died in the box," Hodge continued, drawing the tablet back to her side of the table. "It turns out argon will suffocate a young one. She's pissed at Oddjob for it. She says he should have known that. Oddjob doesn't give a fuck what she thinks. I love that guy, the king of indifference."

"Lefty?" Beck asked, refilling his mug.

"His real name is Abdulaziz something. So, to simplify, your racist, sexist team calls him Lefty. Freya took his right hand at the elevator, remember."

"Racist? Sexist? What?" Beck needed more coffee.

"Oddjob, because he looks like that guy in the James Bond movie. Chan, Charlie Chan. Another movie Asian played by a white guy. Shack, because he's the only black guy on the team. Beeker? Really for the lab guy. Silk? One more comment about lingerie and someone's losing a tooth."

"Did you know Snow is what Yuki's first name means in English?" Beck said. "What's really bothering you? It can't be dumbass nicknames."

She nodded.

11. ONE THEORY AT A TIME

The prisoner woke up, and "Good Morning America" was almost over. He was still wearing yesterday's clothes. *I must have fallen asleep watching TV again last night.* Glancing over, his breakfast was already there. His cell was the same as every other day.

It was a big breakfast today. Two sausage, egg, and cheese sandwiches and hashbrowns like McDonald's. A whole carton of OJ as well.

He was thirsty.

He went for the OJ first, ignoring his headache.

The TV talk show hosts mentioned hangovers. It felt like a hangover. He laughed it off.

He didn't notice the puncture in his arm.

***

"I've been part of giant political machines my entire life," Hodge began. "I feel like a tool here more than ever."

"What do you mean?" Beck asked from the bedroom as he pulled on clean clothes.

"It was too easy to find these assholes." She pushed her cup away. "Do you even know who Sloan takes direction from? Ever wonder?"

"I've been here about twelve hours longer than you, Hodge," Beck said.

"Put your shoes on, and we'll walk Freya before she pisses in here," Hodge said, stopping him from putting on his headset. She also purposefully set her smartphone on the table. Beck got the hint.

It was always warmer at this airport. The tarmac retained the heat and melted the snow. The hangar was set apart from the others, and the hundred yards to the next hangar was filled with small privately owned planes like Cessna 150s. The hangars were good windbreaks for the small planes.

Hodge let Freya off the leash, and she proceeded to pee every hundred feet of sniffing.

Hodge put her arm around Beck's waist as they walked in a very intimate way that didn't match her words.

"I think all the RVs are bugged." She rested her head on his shoulder as they whispered in the breeze. "I think the fucking headsets are also monitored full-time. And as soon as that app is installed on our phones, it will be there also."

"How do you know?" Beck said, pausing as the dog ran off energy in a circle around them.

"A feeling. Easy enough to test," she said. "Just because you're paranoid doesn't mean they're not listening."

"OK. What's the plan?" Beck asked.

"We pretend we are having an affair but be very discrete. See who notices and how. We continue independent research. Don't rely on the team. Crunch our own data. Missing persons was a good place to start. But we have a new variable. They're kidnapped, not killed. What about the 70,000 unidentified bodies annually? There are 600,000 missing persons reported in the US every fucking year."

"There are crazy stories, like UFO abductions," Beck said. "People have blackouts, lose time."

"Outside the box," she said.

"And report none of it. See if they say anything," Beck said as she looked up at him with a glance back at the hangar.

"I also know a guy." And she kissed him. Full and deep.

"You coulda warned me," Beck said. "I haven't been kissed like that for seventeen years."

I have NEVER been kissed like that before...

"You were a priest that long? Good," she said as she separated to put the leash on the dog. "Let's go to Police HQ for the first test."

"Hey," Beck said as he gently touched her face. "I am not sure I was ever enough of a priest. I'd rather not start something I can't finish." He kissed her just barely.

"My timing always sucks," Hodge said as she reluctantly pulled away.

"Guns, we need to arm up," he said. "Maybe armor, too."

When they entered the hangar, she let Freya off the leash, and the dog ran around the helicopter to the conference table, where Gram and Oddjob had several of the collected firearms on the table.

After receiving a nod of permission, Hodge picked up an advanced KRISS Vector. It had a suppressor, tac-light, laser sight, and an ACOG. Its folding stock and single-point sling made it compact and reasonably easy to conceal under a winter coat.

"These take Glock 21 mags? With those wicked rounds?" Hodge asked.

"Yes, they do. Ever fired one? The .45 ACP bullets are also explosive points," Gram answered.

"Put these two on my tab." Hodge wasn't asking. She pushed one into Beck's chest.

Gram slid a black fanny pack across the table. "Here are four mags with a depleted round every other one in the stack. Twenty-two rounds in each mag. Leave them in the trunk unless shit gets surreal."

Hodge smiled wide at the joke. Gram intended it as one. Shit was already surreal.

They put on their headsets and collected their phones. Hodge showed Beck how to put on the single-point sling when both their headsets came on.

"Off somewhere?" Sloan asked over the headset without announcing who he was.

"Random directions seem to be working so far. Anything new from Dr. Hook or our guest?"

"Not yet. Mostly 'fucked' is what he is figuring out," Sloan said.

"Have Hook find out what the deal is with his skin. He may be willing to talk about that," Beck said.

"Is that important?" Sloan asked.

"It might be," Beck replied as they left the trailer.

They started to load gear into the trunk. Armor, the KRISS carbines. Ammo, water, and dog food.

Freya was already excited to go for a ride.

"First stop is the basement at HQ for some more research. We will check in midday, boss," Hodge said as she pulled out of the airport. "Loose cannons out."

"First, we need breakfast," Beck said. "McDonald's, Dunkin' Donuts, or Chick-fil-A?"

***

The two men walked slowly down the long corridor. All the light came from the glass wall on the left. The people that occupied the cells couldn't see or hear them. Most prisoners just watched TV.

"Good stock is getting harder to find," the shriveled old man told Page. "Kapelos was our best supplier. A few months in his shipping containers make this seem like a luxury. And they're satisfied with hot meals, snacks, and all the TV they want."

They paused in front of a cell where the occupant was screaming and slamming his head on the clear wall. Page touched one of the controls on the panel. His screaming stopped. He slowly collapsed to the floor and pissed his already filthy sweat suit.

"You see the difference between this one and this next one. A Kapelos pick." They paused and watched her channel surf. "The voice control came to her easily. The addition of an overstuffed chair and ottoman helped immensely with this type."

"This one would have been culled today. But with Kapelos gone, we will need to…" Page was cut off by the old man.

"Was it him, or were your new dogs just lucky?"

"We've no evidence that Valmunin was involved."

"FIND HIM! You saw that video. You saw how strong he was. You know more than anyone how much blood is required to maintain that prowess. He is feeding at a ferocious rate. Even MORE than you. FIND HIM!"

His raised voice echoed down the dozens of corridors, each lined with cells.

***

It was the last delivery of the day, and it was only 7:36 a.m. Pamela Sikes rolled away from the restaurant, DeWalt's

Fishery. She loved to go there but couldn't afford to very often.

At the corner, she stopped, and when she looked both ways, she finally noticed him sitting in the passenger seat.

"Shit!" she yelled. "Don't do that!"

"Do what?" he said mildly. "I've done nothing."

"You scared the fuck out of me…again." She sighed and moved the truck as the horns started blaring.

"That wasn't scary." Valmunin smiled. "I can be scary."

"Like that smile, it's even scarier," Sikes said. "Haircut helps, though." She kept driving.

"Need your help again," he said. "After your shift."

"Shift's over now, as soon as I get the truck back."

"No ice today?" he asked.

"No, not until tomorrow." Sikes looked at him again. Humor was gone from his face.

"I will meet you in the clinic. When you're ready," Valmunin said.

She didn't see him hop out. She just heard the door slam closed.

Sikes arrived and turned the truck back over with the signed paperwork. The elevator down seemed to go extra slow. As she drifted by the dojo floor, it looked more crowded, not less than the evening session she preferred.

Master Takashi was not there.

The lift stopped on the next level down, and she could hear coughing from the clinic as she walked the hall.

Valmunin was leaning over a stainless-steel sink, coughing. He was shirtless with six fresh bullet wounds on his back and one on the back of his thigh.

Another cough caused a thunk in the sink. It was a large caliber bullet. It was fully mushroomed.

"That's the last of these. The doc doesn't get in until nine." He wiped his mouth before chugging a liter bottle of blood from the open cabinet in front of him now. "I need you to dig this last one out. I can't reach it."

"You've ruined your new jeans already," Sikes said, trying to make light and almost pulling it off. "Sit on this stool. Let's take care of these first."

The drawers were well labeled, and she found gloves and medical adhesive. She wasn't sure the alcohol was necessary, but she didn't ask. In short order, she had all the wounds closed.

"OK, take off your pants," she ordered. "This isn't how I thought this would go the first time."

The wound was worse than she initially thought. The bullet had hit his femur, doing no damage to it. Part of it exited, and a lone large piece was still in there. She had to cut it out. The wound kept closing before she was done. Medical adhesives seemed unnecessary, but closed the six-inch incision up tight.

Sikes helped him put his pants back on, but his shirt was in rags. She helped him to the lift and down, but he was walking easily unassisted by the time he got to the door. A circle of dogs surrounded them. Valmunin paused and said to them. "This is Sikes. Sikes is a friend. Say something so they can hear your voice."

"Well, hello there. Aren't you big fellas?" Sikes said. They all sat in unison. "You can't always keep them down here in the dark."

"No, I don't. They spend most of the time on the roof, training." The door slid open, and they went in. The door slid closed silently behind them.

There was no obvious means to open it.

Valmunin was already in the bedroom and undressing. He crawled into bed unassisted. "Alexa, turn bedroom lights off."

***

They got to the tiny office in records to find a printer had been installed. It sat on top of the file cabinets above the desk. Other typical office supplies were in an open-top box on the desk—notepads, pens, stapler, staples, paperclips, and other stuff.

"Thank you, Betty." Hodge sat and slid her card into the side of the board. Then she noticed a drawer was partially opened.

"Beck, was the door locked?" she asked.

"Yes. I'm sure there are lots of keys. Your Snickers are safe. Want one? I'm having one. Can't remember the last time I had one."

"Sure. Thanks." She was doing the universal *Shhhh*, one finger in front of her lips. She held up a device in the other hand. A Post-it on it simply said, "You'll figure it out."

She was already searching for it by the manufacturer make and model number on Amazon.

It was a thermal scanner used by professional home inspectors. It sold for $6,200. It could detect temp ranges from -32 to 560 F.

Beck took off the Post-it and turned the scanner on. It gave a message that simply said CALIBRATED.

The display showed the walls, floor, and cabinets as green and Freya as oranges, yellows, and reds. When he pointed it at Hodge, it outlined her and indicated *Human*.

He silently handed it to Hodge, and she pointed it at him. Her eyebrows went up, showing she understood its function.

"You think Freya needs a walk?" Beck asked.

"Not now. Let her sleep." Hodge turned off the device and slid it into her pocket. "We'll walk her at lunch. For now, I'm taking a different angle. There's a category called 'unattended death' cross-referenced with the cause of death, 'natural causes' and 'no autopsy.' *Think like your target* was a mantra in our office."

"So you're thinking… like elderly people. Or people at risk of one thing or another. My uncle Dan died like that. Found in his recliner with the TV on. He'd been there a couple days."

"Shit, 6,231 people," she said. "What would you do? Off the top of your head."

"How much blood can you lose, die, and still have enough not to make anyone wonder?" Beck said. "Like a gallon. It wouldn't be listed as a cause of death. If they were at risk like Uncle Dan."

"Gotta find a pattern," she said. "Think supply chain. That Kapelos case has me thinking we've been looking at this all wrong. *What if* with me, man."

"What if they aren't Jack the Ripper types? More like Kapelos."

They were quiet for a while as she crossed referenced what she'd found.

"Should we put Brick on this?" Beck asked.

"You got anything better to do? Outside the box, man. The Entenmann trailer is the biggest box I know right now. New thinking."

Beck took a pad and pen. He wrote *Ask Kapelos?*

She wrote, *Ask me to dinner—the sushi place.*

"Want to go out somewhere to dinner tonight? Sushi maybe? I hear Sakura is good," Beck said.

"Do we need to talk about the Kiss?" She surprised him. "Let's talk about it at dinner. Maybe at my place after."

"Look, Hodge. I've been a priest for the last 15 years," Beck said, honestly nervous. "I'd disappoint you."

"I'll be the judge of that," Hodge said. "I'm usually the disappointer. Don't steal my job."

She wrote on the notepad: *I'm testing a theory.*

Beck wrote below that, *About me, the team, or them?*

She wrote, *Yes.*

***

They data crunched and brainstormed until lunch. Freya wolfed a bowl of kibble and another of water in the garage by the car's open trunk. They reported in and gave Sloan an overview but no specifics.

They had tacos for lunch in a park. While they were chatting, Hodge slid a small case out of her backpack. It looked like a plastic and foam-lined handgun case. She took off her headset and placed her phone in the case. She gestured for Beck to do the same while they were talking about playing chess.

When she snapped the case closed, she whispered in his ear. "I think a Stage One is planted in the night shift at the Underwood nursing home. Six hundred percent more unattended deaths on his shift than any other."

"Will we visit him next?" Beck said. "Maybe test our new gift?"

"In the morning after his shift," Hodge smiled.

"Why keep this quiet?" Beck whispered, close to her ear. *Her hair smells amazing.*

"Testing one theory at a time," she whispered back.

"What theory is that?" he asked, still close.

"Just how long will you stay that close to me?" she said.

He drew back slowly, enjoying the look in her eyes.

She opened the case and put the headset back in her ear. Beck did the same.

***

Back at work, they continued to brainstorm.

They came up with a list of things to find out.

- What happens to the blood drained in funeral homes?
- How do blood donation centers work? Private, not Red Cross.
- What about other kinds of blood?

Beck had this weird feeling that while they were brainstorming, they were also play-acting for some invisible foe who was listening.

Is this how paranoid people feel all the time?

"What if they… what if the team has been looking in the wrong places all this time?" Hodge said. "There are entire industries around human blood collection, uses, and distribution. Not crime, commerce."

"Is it even illegal to drink blood?" Beck asked.

"Depends on where you are. It's considered medical waste in most jurisdictions if it's not collected under specific sterile conditions. Who collects medical waste? Who disposes of the blood past its shelf life? What is the shelf life for consuming it?"

"Let's not cast this net too wide," Beck said. "But bookmark that. Are you hungry for sushi yet?"

She logged off, grabbed her ID, and said, "There are only two great things that taste as good as sushi, and one of them is sushi."

It was a grenade joke, but Beck got it after a minute.

12. HODGE'S APARTMENT

Sloan entered the lab trailer. The back half behind the glass had three bodies on stainless tables in various stages of disassembly. The lights were bright. The Stage Two vampire was heavily strapped to a special gurney. It was propped at 45 degrees. Even the head and torso were under restraints. His head was immobilized with straps, and there were noise-canceling headphones over his ears.

The most disturbing thing to Sloan was that his eyes were also taped closed. The vampire was currently being force-fed.

It was a nightmare.

The doctor was just removing the feeding wedge from between the vampire's teeth.

"Uncover his eyes," Sloan ordered her. "I need to talk to him."

"His skin is like paper," the doctor said. "I'll be careful."

The medical tape did, in fact, create a small rip in his skin above one eyebrow. The bright lights made him squeeze his eyes shut. The doctor took off the headphones.

"Can you hear me, Mr. Kapelos?" said Sloan. "My name is Six, and this is Dr. Hook. Can you understand me?"

"I understand you. Fucker. It's you that needs to understand me. I'm going to kill you and everyone you ever cared about," Kapelos growled.

"Mr. Kapelos, I think you underestimate the depth of your predicament. I've never had a vampire as active as you at my mercy. As Dr. Hook can attest, I've very little mercy. This is standard protocol to control a prisoner such as yourself. Others have described the sensation as being sealed in a block of cement. Ironically, it's how we disposed of him. He was sealed in a block of cement, with no arms or legs, just his face exposed. In the dark, the quiet." Sloan's tone was even and calm, making it more frightening. "The mistake we made that first time was to encase his anus. He only lasted four years, vomiting and nearly drowning in his own guano. Disgusting, really, so we covered the rest in cement and dropped him in the ocean."

Kapelos's eyes were wide now.

"As fun as that was, I'd rather be friends, Mr. Kapelos. You see, I'm the most merciful one here. Dr. Hook wants to dissect you alive under a microscope. Others want to drown you, head first, twice daily, every day, in a septic tank in New Jersey. Have you ever been to Jersey?"

Dr. Hook finally spoke. "Whatever you decide, your old life is over. We killed your three minions. They'll keep me happy for a good while. We could starve you and see how long that takes. Decapitate you and see how long your brain lasts. We actually have a guillotine we've never used. We know your bones are like iron, well, not *like* they *are* iron. That's also why I'll take your limbs at the sockets. Easier."

"You people are monsters," he said with fear in his voice.

"Yes, Mr. Kapelos. Monsters… not cattle."

***

Hodge and Beck stumbled into Hodge's apartment but didn't turn on the lights. She laughed and giggled as she struggled to get her backpack off. She crashed into a table, and a lamp toppled and crashed.

"Oops." She pushed Beck back until he sat in an armchair. She held her fingers over his lips and said, "Stay here. I'll be right back." She pulled one of the suppressed KRISS carbines out of her backpack and pressed him back into his chair with it against his chest.

As an afterthought, she kissed him in the dark. "I'll be right back." She took out the other carbine and placed it in the other chair.

He watched her unmake and tangle up the bed in the city lights that came in the windows. She arranged pillows that looked like two people embraced. She sat in the other chair.

"Hodge is signing out 10-7. Call the cell in an emergency," she said and gestured to him. The only reply was a double click—standard acknowledgment.

"Beck is 10-7. Goodnight, Coffee."

"Goodnight, sir." Coffee was still on duty.

Without thinking, he spoke out loud as he took off his earpiece. "I swear Coffee never sleeps."

"Don't worry about Freya. She's fine in the car, in the garage, for the night. Now shut up and kiss me, dumbass," she said, and they fell silent. She sat back in her chair without kissing him.

The sounds of the building became the world all around. They sat in deep shadows.

The apartment was quiet for two hours. They didn't have to wait long.

Sounds at the front door proved to be lock picks. The door opened and closed silently. The movement was revealed by light from the hall. It showed a man dressed in dark clothes with an HK MP5 on a sling.

He stealthily walked into the trap.

He was perfectly silhouetted in the arch of the open French doors as he took aim. Suppressed, full auto gunfire tore through the bed. When he was removing the mag and replacing it, Hodge opened fire, and Beck followed.

The first four shots were in the man's back, and he turned toward the darkened room as if he hadn't felt them.

Hodge and Beck both made headshots. He toppled onto the ruined bed.

They stood and covered the door and the windows. For thirty seconds, they listened to their headset squawking. Both their phones were buzzing.

Beck picked up his headset and put it on. "Beck, status," said Coffee's voice.

"Stage Two down," Beck said. "I'm getting sick of this shit."

"I need a vacation," Hodge said. She was holding the thermal device, pointing it at the body on the bed. The body was at room temperature. The MP5 was hot red and yellow.

"Tell Hook, this one was harder to drop. Might be more than a Two," Beck said as he moved to the window. "Shit, cops are pulling up to the building across the street."

"Fuck. These armor-piercing rounds are going to be hard to explain," Hodge said.

"The report is shattered windows in the building across the street. No injuries," Coffee said. "What's the damage there?"

"Four tiny holes in the wall over the bed. The bed is torn up. Thirty-three rounds on full auto," Hodge said. "Probably standard rounds."

"Was it loud?" Sloan asked.

"What?" Beck let slip out. Making a nervous joke.

"Will your neighbors call 911, or will you have time?" Sloan asked.

"Time, I think. I know where you're going. Team ETA?" she said as she let the KRISS swing around to her back and unmade the bed. She tossed pillowcases at Beck first.

"ETA 9 minutes," Oddjob answered.

Beck pulled the two pillowcases over the dead guy's head. There wasn't much blood. They rolled him in the sheets and quilts from the bed.

"That was my fucking grandmother's quilt," Hodge said.

"ETA 3 minutes," Oddjob updated.

"Park by elevator two on level P3," Hodge said. "In the handicapped spot."

"Cameras?" Sloan asked.

"There are cameras, but they don't work. Placebo," Hodge said. "Let us know when you're there. We'll bring him down and roll."

She came out of the kitchen with a roll of duct tape. The body was wrapped and taped when Oddjob, Tank, Chan, and Beeker arrived. She quickly looked around the apartment, and they left.

Hodge pressed the elevator call button. It almost opened right away. Beck carried the heavy body over and propped it upright in the corner. He placed his back to it to hold it up. His KRISS carbine was low-ready. Hodge pressed P3, and the doors closed. The numbers counted down in slow motion from fifteen. At six, they felt it stop and heard a ding.

An oblivious young woman stepped in and pressed G. She had bright pink headphones on with cat ears and never looked up from her phone. She got out on the ground floor into the lobby. The doorman must have waved because she waved to him.

On P3, Beeker was waiting at the door in an EMT uniform. Tank had on the same. There was an open ambulance right there, gurney waiting. They saw Freya alert in the back when moving to their unmarked patrol car.

"I want to see you two in my office now. If not sooner," Sloan said.

***

There was a tiny office in the front of the command trailer that the crew called the ready room. It was supposed to be Sloan's office but was rarely used that way. It had a couch that the command crew would nap on during long shifts.

Beck and Hodge entered the office, and before Beck could close the door, Hodge was at parade rest in front of Sloan's desk like she was ready for a formal dress-down.

"Report," Sloan barked.

"First, I need to show you this." She slipped her backpack off and took out the handgun case. She removed her headset and placed it and her phone in the Faraday case. Beck followed suit. After hesitating, Sloan followed as well.

"What. The. Fuck. Is this about?" Sloan said in a near whisper.

Hodge leaned in and rested her palms on the desk. Beck came closer. Hodge's KRISS carbine bumped the desk as if for emphasis before she began.

"I believe our comms are compromised," she whispered, looking at Beck. "Tonight was a test, and we set a trap. It would either be a sleepless night or proof. If it's you that's compromised, we're fucked either way. I also believe whoever compromised our comms has been compromised by someone else."

Hodge drew out the thermal image device. She brought up a still image of a body on the floor at room temp. A dotted outline of the body was tagged with 'V-72.285F.' *Vampire.* She held it up and took an image of Beck. He was also outlined but tagged 'H-97.9155F'. *Human.*

"Call a mandatory all-hands meeting. Get them out of bed if you need to," Hodge said. "Beck put Freya in the Winnebago. If this goes how I think it will, I don't want her ripping any arms off. Yet."

They all took their headsets and phones back.

"And one more thing, where did you really get the dog?" Sloan was surprised when Beck replied.

"The same place I got this." He held up the thermal scanner.

Hodge was checking her mag load as they left the office.

"Coffee, call a mandatory All-Hands. I want everyone around that conference table in five minutes." Sloan stepped out of the office. "Even you."

"Yes, sir."

"Gram, bring me one of those AR10s with a mag of depleted rounds. I need to talk about them with the crew. We found out something," Sloan said over the comms.

Gram was one of the first to fall in. She handed the heavy rig to Sloan and took her place. Everyone was seated in three minutes.

Casually, Sloan chambered a round. It was loud in the quiet hanger. He looked at everyone around the table. Hodge started scanning as he spoke, starting at the end where the command crew sat. Coffee, Brick, Book, and Snow were first. All glowed warm.

"Everyone knows that shit's been crazy since Beck joined in," Sloan said. "I thought Switch was a hot eleventh man. But

Jesus Christ. He should have had someone to cover his back. That position will now be permanent on the team."

Hodge paused briefly with the scanner and placed its lanyard around her neck before she continued. She casually showed Sloan the scanner and let it drop to hang by the lanyard.

Sloan, Hodge, and Beck stood behind their empty chairs with weapons at low ready.

"We've also discovered that we have a leak," he said, and all three aimed directly at Dr. Hook. "Doctor, move an inch, and you'll lose your head. Gram, collar, please."

"What are you saying?" Franklin spoke. "Six, please. Let me explain."

The rest of the team all drew side arms and backed away from her. Beck left the table.

"Oh, you'll do a lot of explaining," said Sloan.

He and Oddjob bent her over the conference table as he clamped manacles on her wrists behind her back and pulled her neck back by a handful of hair.

Gram clamped a thick collar on her neck.

"That collar on your neck is packed with very high explosives, all aimed inward. If you get too far from the transmitter or try to take it off, it will explode. Cause any trouble, and I can also manually trigger it."

Oddjob forced her into a chair.

Beck came back with Freya on the leash. She instantly tensed and began to growl low when brought into the circle. Then she pointed at Franklin and lifted her right paw. Beck led her out again, back to the RV, and quickly returned.

"You have to let me explain…" She was sobbing now.

"I should have known," Beck said. "I had just recently read your file. There are photos of you in there. They're all like this."

Beck scattered a dozen photos of Franklin from her file. They all showed a frumpy, overweight, middle-aged woman, not the lean and fit woman restrained before them now.

"You have to listen. Yes. It's true. I'm one *now*." She was frantic. "But I would never betray the team. I was dying. I had a kind of leukemia. I would have been dead already. I didn't know what would happen. But I lived. Then I didn't know what to do. I told Switch. I asked him what I should do. He said to keep quiet for now. I documented the effects. You gotta believe me. I never killed anyone." She was confessing in a flood.

"I should have known, dammit," Beeker chimed in. "She was going through a lot of blood 'studies.' I'm a fucking idiot."

Franklin was crying now, sobbing uncontrollably.

"How did you deal with the eye problem?" Beck asked. "It's always really bright in the lab."

Franklin was obvious in her desperate cooperation. "I wear contact lenses. They are brown-eyed with a fixed iris because mine are wide open. I knew it would be a problem, so I ordered them in advance." She was pleading to Beck now and not Sloan. "It's all in my notes on my laptop. It's never connected to the network. It's in the cold room. The drawer in the last table."

Hodge disappeared into the lab and appeared with the laptop and power cord. She opened it on the table. "Password?"

"Capital R, Revelation166." Her sobbing renewed.

"I didn't know you were religious," Sloan said.

Beck replied from memory. "Revelation 16:6—For they have shed the blood of saints and prophets, and thou hast given them blood to drink; for they are worthy."

"I'm in," Hodge said.

"Well, you're the eleventh man," Sloan said to Beck. "I think we need another random direction. What do you recommend?"

Everyone was looking at Beck. He hesitated only for a moment.

"Every asset needs to be searched and scanned for bugs, or better yet, sold off and replaced. All phones and comm gear, replaced." Beck took off his headset and tossed it along with his phone on the table. Without being asked, Hodge did the same.

"Fuck." Coffee ripped his headset off next and tossed it on the table. "It'll be faster to scrap and rebuild. Do we have budget for that?"

"Yes. And in cash, no paper trails," Sloan replied. "We are now officially on a comms BLACKOUT. Anyone so much as calls their momma, and I will kill you myself."

"I want $200,000 in a duffle. Hodge and I leave here in 15 minutes with Franklin and Kapelos in the ambulance. You want random, you get random."

A flurry of activity ensued. The power was cut to the entire hangar. Batteries were disconnected from all the vehicles. Computers were unplugged. The ambulance was loaded with weapons and supplies, and the two vampires bound on gurneys. Oddjob ripped the radios and computers out of the ambulance and did a bug sweep.

Hodge and Beck emerged from the RV dressed in hospital scrubs.

"I need one more of the team to help us." Beck looked over the team and said, as they were about to leave. "Snow. You're with us. Your chopper will be the hardest to search. It will take Coffee the longest. You're with us."

Hodge tossed her some scrubs. "Change into these. Leave everything. Watch, jewelry, everything." To Beck's surprise, Snow began to strip right there. She even tossed her underwear into the pile.

After she was dressed, Beck told her, "You'll drive." He tossed the keys to Snow.

Sloan handed Beck a business card. On the back was an email address and password. "When you're ready, find an open terminal like a library or Internet café. Log into this email address. Write an email and save it as Draft. Don't send it. When I log in and read it, I will delete it without sending it. No emails to intercept, no trace routes."

"Use a browser that supports Incognito Mode," Beck whispered as he checked that a round was chambered in his Desert Eagle.

"Weren't you a priest last week?" Sloan smiled.

"Yeah, I'm just feeling a bit more Old Testament this week," Beck said as he settled the lab coat better to hide his shoulder holster.

***

Hodge rode in the back of the ambulance. The prisoners were bound heavily and strapped to gurneys. She had her KRISS carbine trained on Franklin's head. Her back was to the opening of the cab. Freya sat in the far back of the ambulance at full alert. Both prisoners had their eyes bandaged closed and wore noise-canceling headphones. Ball gags were around their necks if needed, and they knew it.

Beck spoke as they exited the airport. "Snow, where can we quietly get a chopper?"

13. THE BLOOD HERETIC

Mr. Page was shown into the massive library in the Lodge. A fire was roaring in the oversized ornate hearth.

Lord Aelfric Tauler slouched in an oversized wingback chair with a book open in his lap. He spoke so softly, Page barely heard the words.

"How does he remain so…" he paused, searching for words. "…immune to time? His prowess seems prescient."

"I've studied the video closely from last night's trap. He was shot at least six times, maybe more. He doesn't even seem to notice."

"The new in the clan overestimate their new abilities." Page began from parade rest. "They only compare themselves to humans."

"His sword work speaks of the Far East," Lord Tauler said. "A part of the world closed to us for centuries."

"There's something else, my lord," Page said humbly.

"What is it?" Tauler looked up.

"The dogs have slipped the chain," Page said. "They were ready for our visit. They have Kepelos alive. Or at least what's left of him. They seem to be hunting on their own. We can't have them disrupting our operations."

"What are you saying?" Tauler was angry. It radiated from him like heat.

"Perhaps it would be wise to relocate to the mountain." Page was staying calm.

"You know how I hate the cold."

"The facility has been modernized since you were there last. It doesn't have the farm capacity of the Lodge, but it's safer," Page recommended.

"For hundreds of years, we were without a single threat in all the world. Until Valmunin turned on us all." Tauler looked into the fire. "In the single greatest heresy, he began to drink the blood of his peers."

Page was taken aback. It was the greatest evil in all the world, akin to being a cannibal among humans.

"The Blood Heretic shall be stopped. Equilibrium will be restored." Page let his own anger seep through his words.

***

The ambulance followed a rusty gray van into the employee parking lot of the Bayshore Regional Sewage Authority. They parked side by side in the back of the lot.

Snow, Beck, and Hodge transferred the prisoners from the ambulance to the van. In two minutes, they were again on the move.

"Why switch vehicles?" Snow asked. She was driving again.

"Just being paranoid. The ambulance may have a tracker." Beck replied. "Now we need a chopper. Where can you get one off books, Snow? Your file says you're resourceful."

"For how long? How far are you going?" Snow asked as if she was already considering options.

"Three hours," Beck replied. "Round trip. First, we need to stop at Keansburg Outfitters."

"The closest one is on Rt 36. It's about 10 minutes from here," Hodge said.

They were in and out in less than 30 minutes. They carried a lot of packages: gear they might need and new gear they were sure had no tracking devices.

"Chopper next?" Snow asked.

"Affirmative," Beck replied.

They drove another fifteen minutes to a place called Ideal Beach. It was far from ideal. But two blocks off the beach was a helicopter flight school, New York City Tours, and Air Taxi business.

"I know the owner. He was my first flight instructor. Nice old hippie kinda dude. When he was 19, he was flying Hueys in Vietnam." Snow drove right out onto the tarmac and parked adjacent to an MH-65 Dolphin helicopter that had seen better days. It was painted with gray primer and had poorly added tail numbers.

Snow reached into Beck's duffle and came out with a bundle of cash. She held it up to Beck, and he just nodded. She climbed out of the van and ran toward the low building with peeling white paint. Before she arrived, an old man with a white Santa beard came out holding a shotgun.

Snow hugged him around the neck and spoke to him briefly, handing him the bundle of cash. He kissed her forehead and went back inside without another glance.

Snow returned and opened a side compartment to retrieve the ignition key to the chopper on top of the battery.

"Let's load 'em up," Beck said.

In the air, Snow finally asked, "OK. Where to?"

"Do you remember that oil rig?" Beck replied.

***

Valmunin watched her carefully climb out of bed and tiptoe to the bathroom. He could see her in the dark. The clock said it was 4:11 p.m. He heard the shower turn on, and after a moment, he got up.

"Alexa, turn Morning on," Val said to the room, and gently, the lights rose to a warm morning glow.

He walked to the vast bathroom naked. The shower was so oversized it was the entire far end of the room. Tiled benches were on three sides, and Sikes sat on one, leaning forward, rinsing the soap from her hair. She tilted her head to the side and saw him.

He smiled and entered the shower on the far end. His back was to her. He reached back and removed a bandage that he could reach and rinsed off the now-healed spot.

"Here. Let me," Sikes said and collected the other six and joined Val in washing them with Ivory soap. "Don't get any ideas. My legs are still shaky from last night."

"I live to serve," Valmunin said in a way that made her insides tremble. He washed her from the feet up. Her snake tattoo began on the top of her left foot and wound up around her calf and then her thigh. Up across her hip and belly below her navel, around her back along the side of her left breast, along her collarbone, and up her neck to whisper in her ear.

He traced the entire length of that snake. It was beautiful in its artistry. Its colors and dimension made it seem to move with her as he dried her.

From a peg on the wall, he wrapped her in an oversized black terrycloth robe.

"Help yourself to breakfast," Valmunin said. "I'll be out in a minute."

"Can I make you anything?" she asked.

"I'll show you when I come out." He kissed her head and walked to the closet.

Sikes was sitting on the kitchen's black and red granite island with a glass of orange juice and buttered toast when he came in wearing another black terrycloth robe. His bare feet were silent on the hardwood floor.

"Where's Aiko? Doesn't she feed the dogs?" Sikes asked.

"About that." Valmunin opened a cabinet and took out a large porcelain bottle with Japanese glyphs. "She's gone. I'd like to offer you her position."

"What did she do around here?" Sikes asked.

"Anything she wanted. Everything," he said with an odd tone she'd never heard. "She trained the dogs. She lived here. She took care of me. Kept my secrets." He poured a thick liquid like honey into a tall coffee mug.

"Do I look like a maid to you?" she said, offense slipping into her voice.

"Aiko was no more a maid than you are now. She was my teacher. My protector when I sleep. My advisor. My friend. By the way, I make my own bed."

"What's the pay?" she asked. "Is room and board included?"

"How much do you want?

"Do I have to take care of all those dogs?"

"The dogs all went with her," Val explained. "Winter is not the best for them in this city."

"I made $18 an hour as the delivery driver."

"How about $100,000 a year," Valmunin said, causing her eyebrows to go up.

"I'm not a whore." Sikes was emphatic.

"I'm never paying for that," he said so gently she paused.

"What's the most difficult part of this job?" she asked, getting back on track.

"Now, that's a good question. Come, follow me." Valmunin got up, took his mug, and moved through the great room to a wall of Japanese sliding panels. He opened them, and lights slowly came up inside.

Three redwood hot tubs were there. He pressed a wall control, and their covers retracted.

"Without these, I couldn't walk among mankind," Valmunin began. "This first one is a specific set of oils that keep my skin like this. This second one is a complex blend of herbs. I've no idea what's in there, but it allows me to sleep, to easily manually control the irises in my eyes, and stops the lesions and hair loss that plague my kind. Never go in this one. What's good for me in this case could kill you."

"And what's in this one?" Sikes asked.

"Saline with the same salt content as your body," Valmunin said. "You'll enjoy the first and third."

"So, it will be my job to maintain these? How?" Sikes asked.

"All you need to know is in that book on the podium." He pointed to the far end of the room. That wall was lined with dark, lacquered cabinets, and the open book.

He took off his robe and climbed into the third tub. He held out his hand, and she followed suit and joined.

"Hell of an interview, man," she said. "You gotta know up front. I don't like doing it in a hot tub. I get too sore."

"Wait until you try the hot oil tub…"

***

The chopper skimmed just above the waves to avoid conventional radar. They were running dark with no transponder beacons and not even running lights.

The flashing lights of the former oil rig were visible on the corners and transmission tower—no other lights shown. The sun was below the horizon, but the twilight sky was still bright, providing a silhouette of the massive abandoned structure.

It had three helipads in a diagonal line, and they landed on the center one. As the engine spun down, Snow was describing the facility.

"An array of solar panels runs all the lights and typical living spaces. The rig also has six big diesel generators that all worked, last I knew. They're way overpowered because all the equipment they used to run is gone. The furnace was set at 50 degrees to keep it from freezing. All that shit is obvious in the control room. It's made for idiots to be able to monitor."

Hodge showed her the sat phone they bought at the outfitters. "I will call and leave a message for you at your sister's when we need to get picked up."

"Don't tell a soul about any of this. Not even Sloan," Beck said. "Don't say a single word about it out loud. Make a note of anyone that asks."

Snow never got out of the chopper. She and the ambulance would be back at the base in two hours.

∗∗∗

Sloan fumed as he stared at the pile of listening devices that kept growing on the conference table. Every RV, tractor, and trailer had at least one.

"These are all burst transmission devices," Coffee said to Sloan as he dropped two more on the table. "We call them 'garage door openers' because a standard bug sweep won't find them. They never transmit until they receive a go-code. Shit, boss. A passing chopper taking off or landing could send the signal and collect the data. Hell, a guy on a passing motorcycle.

A bicycle!”

Sloan saw that Coffee was getting spun up. He knew Coffee was taking it personally. It was one of his jobs to conduct bug sweeps and monitor IP activity on the network.

“Is there any way you can find out who this was being sent to?” Sloan asked.

“No. These things are point-to-point only. They have a limited transmission range. They only communicate with the proximity device. That device plugs into a laptop. Maybe if we had that thing, it’s pocket size. It looks like a remote control.”

“Search the lab and Franklin’s RV. Fine. Tooth. Comb,” Sloan said.

Oddjob walked up as Coffee was stepping into the lab.

“Six, we should evac. Pull back to the Wilkes-Barre industrial complex. I’m feeling crosshairs.” Oddjob was scowling. “Let the Vs kill each other for a while.”

Sloan looked at the pile of bugs on the table. He scanned all the vehicles. His eyes finally rested on the chopper.

“We’ll wait until Snow gets back. That’s a two-hour drive from here, and I would like some air support if we convoy on Rt. 80,” Sloan decided. “Destroy these and toss them in the river.” He gestured to the bugs with his chin.

“Yes, sir.” Oddjob started piling them into an ammo can. He added some gasoline to the can and tossed in a match as Coffee walked up with another bug. The smoke was minimal.

“Excellent.” He tossed it into the fire and began to move toward Franklin’s RV.

“Do you think it was Ponytail that did this? He knew about the cams,” Sloan asked.

Coffee stopped and turned back, thinking.

Oddjob replied. “No. This was something else.”

***

The temp inside the rig was about 50 degrees Fahrenheit. It was way colder on the helipad in the December winds. It only took them thirty minutes to situate the gurneys into two separate rooms in the base infirmary.

"OK, man," Hodge said to Beck. "What's the plan here?"

"We get what we can from Kapelos. If he doesn't cooperate, he goes over the side. Metal gurney and all. He'll have an hour to think about it."

"And Franklin?" Hodge asked as she found a bowl for dog food.

"That's a longer question. We only have six units of blood with us," Beck replied. "Let's have a meal and explore the base to see what our resources are, and then we can decide."

They found that the huge commercial kitchen was still well stocked with canned and dried foods. There were years' worth of beans, rice, and SPAM, but they opted for canned beef stew. The small amount of food in the walk-in fridge had gone bad and was sent down the garbage chute into the ocean. Trash compactors would compress other non-organic trash into blocks for the incinerator.

The freezer held a mystery. There were hundreds of plastic one-quart bottles of blood.

"I thought blood couldn't be frozen," Hodge said. "We will need to ask Franklin."

"No time like the present," Beck said.

Before they removed the eye bandages or noise-canceling headset, Beck hung a unit of blood directly in her field of view.

He uncovered her ears first, and she began begging straight away.

"Silence, or it's the muzzle," Hodge said flatly.

She hushed.

"This is how this will go." Beck began. "We ask questions, and you answer. Failure to answer won't go well for you."

"I understand," she said with a trembling voice as he peeled off the gauze pads taped over her eyes.

"Do you know where you are?" Beck asked, and she looked around.

"No," she replied and added, "You gotta let me tell you what…"

"I warned you…" Beck slapped the bandages back on her eyes and headset back on her ears. He turned up the white noise real loud. And then added the stainless-steel muzzle.

Without a word, he gestured for Hodge to follow, and they went to the next room.

The same procedure was taken with Kapelos, who didn't say a word. But he stared at the unit of blood hanging there.

"As long as you're useful, you'll live. Give us good intelligence, and we will feed you," Beck said.

"What kind of info do you want?" Kapelos asked.

"Initially, I leave that to you," Beck said. "If you don't cooperate, I give you to her."

"OK, OK, OK," Kapelos began. "The oldest V I know of is named Rhys Valmunin. He's a monster. The worst of us. He is powerful and has to consume probably ten times what I do. He even feeds on other vampires. Normal guns won't kill him, not normal bullets." All this came out in a flood.

"What? Like silver bullets?" Beck asked, already knowing.

"No, like super armor-piercing shit."

"Where can we find this Valmunin?" Beck asked.

"In NYC. He's a monster. But he's ancient. His skeleton must be solid iron by now."

"How old are you?"

"202. I was born in 1814. Turned in 1852. Valmunin is like five times older than me."

"What did you do before the parking garage?"

"I was an undertaker," Kapelos said. "It's not as fresh, but in the old days, they wanted them buried quick. The supply was plentiful in cities, and cheap prices kept the supply flowing."

"Do you know any undertakers that are active now?"

"No. But they'd be easy to find. Ones with owner-operators. Especially ones with cheap crematoriums. Drain em and burn em." He was speaking fast, trying to please and staring at the unit of blood. "In poor areas, cremation contracts with prisons and hospitals. Hospitals and prisons have morgues, and the bodies stay fresh longer."

"Why are you talking now and not before?"

"I could tell Franklin had turned. I can smell it," he said. "I thought I would use that info as leverage to escape."

"How did you know we took Franklin?"

"I could smell her, her fear."

"What else can you smell?" Beck asked.

"We are at sea, far from shore. Probably a tanker. I smell oil, and it's big enough for a helipad."

"What do you know about freezing blood?"

"It ruins it," he said. "Trust me, I tried it. Six weeks, tops, is the shelf life if stored correctly."

***

"OK. Let's try this again," Beck said after he took the headphones off Franklin. He tore off the eye bandages but left the steel ball gag. "I ask, and you answer questions."

"I understand," Franklin tried to say around the ball.

Beck used the controls to set her up to a 45-degree angle. He began reviewing her file where she could see. "I don't know if you were aware of this, but as the eleventh man, I have access to ALL the data in your file. These photos alone should have alerted me."

Beck held up a series of photos of Franklin before she'd joined the team. She was thirty pounds overweight and looked very different. "I also have access to your private medical records. Yes, HIPAA be damned. I didn't read them before because I didn't believe it was important, and I respected the team's privacy. Was that only a week ago?"

Franklin said nothing but had begun to cry quietly.

"It says you've Waldenstrom's macroglobulinemia. And your bone marrow is in ruins. And you stopped all treatments." Beck closed the file. "Terminal prognosis. Did it work?"

"Work?" She was confused.

"I presume you did this to yourself. When? Based on your body temperature, it had to be at least a year ago."

"Two. August of 2014," she said, unable to look at him.

"And now it's the winter of 2016. You look better than you ever have in your adult life. I already believe you did this to yourself as a Hail Mary. Tell me the story."

Her crying had started her nose running. Beck released her left hand and gave her a hand towel to get herself together before she began. Hodge unholstered her handgun when he released her hand.

"I had Waldenstrom's for about five years when I joined the team. It was why I had become a blood expert. I didn't want anyone to know. Especially Sloan," she said. "This is what I was trying to tell you. When I came to the team a year or so after, it turned for the worse. We had a Stage Two in the lab. And I did it. I drank its blood. A lot of it." She began to sob again.

"How long before you knew?" Beck asked.

"My laptop has a spreadsheet and log of my transition." She gave the filename and location. "The first symptom was in less than 48 hours—loss of automatic iris reflex. Wide open, normal light became blinding. I've only recently gained minimal conscious control over them."

Beck lifted a light from a nearby tray of items. "May I?" he asked politely as he held up the light. Franklin tried to nod, but her head was secured too well. Beck walked to her right side. When he flashed the light into her pupils, they didn't react.

"I can close them, but it takes a minute." She blinked and focused on the distant ceiling, and the pupils contracted to a small dot in about a minute.

"Then what?"

"Constant hunger that normal food didn't satisfy. I started consuming blood in the lab. I was always doing blood research, just not the kind they thought. No one noticed almost a gallon a week."

"It's all here," Hodge said. "Even the fall in body temperature. It looks like it became room temperature in just under a year."

"You became cold-blooded?" Beck prompted.

"I experimented on body temperature." It was like she was confessing now. "My mind worked better at higher temps. 102 Fahrenheit was optimal. Tough to maintain. I almost quit the team and moved to the southwest."

"Why didn't you? You were on a team of people whose job was to kill you," Hodge asked.

"It was the easy access to… food." She hesitated. "I knew I couldn't kill people for it." She looked at Beck. "And nobody noticed. The rest of the team didn't like me already. I encouraged it. I heard the Franklinstein cracks. So I kept to myself. Plus, Beeker is a lazy dumbass."

"Who were you contacting on the outside?" Beck asked directly.

"No one. I swear." She was pleading. "I lived in constant fear someone would find out. I isolated even more."

"It says in here the Waldenstrom's disappeared," Hodge said.

"Not so much disappeared as was no longer a factor," she said. "Please. You gotta believe me. I never betrayed the team."

"Any idea who did?" Beck asked.

"It may have been… Switch," she answered. "I think… It may be why he was killed. Oddjob never filed a report. Sloan thought he was just upset in his own way."

14. VALMUNIN'S STORY

Sikes spent an hour reading the volume that was titled *The Guidance* as she sat in a comfy chair, still wearing her robe. When she saw Valmunin slowly emerge from the oil, she dropped her robe on the chair.

Valmunin climbed the steps and paused on the top one as the oil ran off his body back into the tub.

Sikes crossed the catwalk behind the tubs and picked up a fine hairbrush on a shelf there as Valmunin turned his back to her.

Sikes began to brush the oil out of his hair.

"I see you've begun reading *The Guidance*." He leaned his head back and used his hands to squeegee oil from his face.

"Aiko was very specific. After brushing your hair, I'm to use the gua sha tool, top down," Sikes said, lifting a dark wooden oval with a flat end. All the edges were rounded.

"Just imagine you're scraping the thick oil back into the tub," Valmunin said as he slowly turned for her.

"*The Guidance* also stated that this had a certain… effect," she said as her hand closed around his slick erection. "Me too."

***

Page gazed out his floor-to-ceiling windows at the Catskill mountains. His mid-century modern home perched on a cliff like a work of art. A tree was perfectly framed in his view like a bonsai with the lake and forests below.

She was thorough as she worked the oil into his skin. She was so good. In fact, he would not eat this one until her skill began to diminish. She was still fit and dressed to his liking. She'd been doing this service almost daily now for a decade or two.

"Sir." Page could only see the man's feet. He understood that it must be important for him to interrupt.

"What is it, Wallace?" Page didn't attempt to get up.

"The surveillance suite has been discovered, the new dogs have disappeared, and the Master wants to see you immediately."

"Fuck." Page began to sit up. The masseuse stopped and took two steps back, dropping her hands to her sides and bowing her head. He sat on the massage table, thinking. Finally, he said to the girl, "Kanryō shimashita." She bowed and shuffled away.

"Sir, what'll you do with her if we are forced to evacuate again?" Wallace held up a robe for Page. He shrugged into it.

"She may be blind, but she is the best masseuse I've had in two centuries." He moved to his closet.

"And if we retreat to the sanctuary while we are elsewhere… This place is now only accessible by air," Wallace said.

"That reminds me. Do the preflight and warm up the helicopter. I leave in fifteen minutes."

***

"Who devised these restraints? Very effective," Kapelos said, looking down at the bindings.

Beck had released his head straps and positioned his gurney at a 45-degree angle. Sitting up, he could drink from the bottle Beck held.

"I think they're based on the only restraints Houdini couldn't escape from," Beck answered. "Now, drink this down. All of it."

Beck held a wide-mouth, quart-sized bottle to his mouth. Kapelos tilted his head back with his mouth open wide. Beck poured the entire bottle in all at once. Kapelos didn't even have to swallow. It just flowed directly down his throat.

He closed his mouth and raised his eyebrows. "That's the good stuff. I was expecting pig's blood. A young girl by the taste. You surprise me."

"You don't know me," Beck replied slightly sinisterly. That meal was for your cooperation thus far. If you ever want more, you'll need to provide additional information."

"What do you want to know?"

"Tell me more about this one you call Valmunin."

"His name is Rhys Valmunin. He was born in Jaeder, Norway, in 960." Kepelos was eager to please. "Eventually, he migrated in 986 to eastern Greenland. He lived in a small Norse village, wedged between the freezing water of a branch of the Isa Fjord and the Gray mountains."

"That's very specific," Hodge said.

"He's a legend. All elders know his story. The village he was from was surrounded by giant forests full of game and enough rocky pasture to support the small fields and flocks of goats. His life was just like his father's and his father's father. These hard and savage times bred hard and savage men. He was a seafaring Norseman in the classic sense. He and his whole village lived on the shattered bones and spilled blood of others.

Women, children, native Americans, and even priests." Kepelos was almost reciting. "Rhys Valmunin was a murderous bastard long before he was turned."

***

Snow rolled into the hangar as the last of the cars were being placed on the enclosed carrier. Her motorcycle was already secured inside her chopper.

Sloan stepped up to Snow. "Status?"

"Are you sure that guy was a priest a week ago?" Snow began. "They're off-grid and in the wind. Being paranoid as fuck. They aren't even wearing the same clothes. We changed vehicles a couple times. I don't know where they're going."

"We are moving to the Wilkes-Barre base. Convoy. You're on air support during the two-hour run. Then you'll fly Oddjob back here to get Beck's RV. Or he will if he comes back here."

"Beck bought a half dozen burner phones. It probably won't be long before you hear from them," Snow said as they moved to the chopper. "Some asshole has been in my cockpit." Her tone was angry.

"My orders. We were searching for bugs and tracking devices. We found several. Though no bugs in the chopper, only a tracker," Sloan said.

"I'll search it myself again when shit quiets down," Snow said as she climbed in.

Sloan moved over to Coffee, who was closing the back of the command trailer. Sloan knew he'd drive that truck. He slept in the sleeper cab of the rig.

"Ready to roll, sir. When we get to the new base, I'll acquire all new cell phones. Until then, we'll use CB radio channel eight on the road."

"Open channel 8?" Sloan asked.

"Yes," Coffee said as he climbed into his cab and put on shades and a trucker cap with a Peterbilt logo. Rolling down the window, he ritually patted a sticker on the door that said, "Ass, Gas, or Grass. Nobody Rides For Free" as the engine fired up.

The helicopter began to spin up.

Sloan was driving his black Chevy Suburban towing his 26-foot Airstream.

He picked up the mic for the little-used CB radio. "And we are off. Radio check."

***

Beck walked into Franklin's area holding another quart of the thawed blood they'd found in the freezer. He loosened the top and handed it to Franklin. Her left hand was still not secured.

She looked at it like it was poisoned.

"It's safe. If I wanted to kill you, I would have just pushed your gurney over the side," Beck said.

Franklin sniffed it, then sipped it. After the initial taste, she up-ended the bottle and drained it fast, as if he might take it from her.

"Thank you," she said, covering her mouth with her hand, knowing her teeth would still be a red mess. "May I have a small glass of water?"

"Sure." There was a water cooler and paper cups nearby. "Why?" He filled a cup and traded it for the plastic bottle.

"If I don't rinse my mouth, my teeth look... it's a mess." Franklin was embarrassed.

"What can you tell me about Dunn & Hammond Polyvinyl Alcohol Crystallization Inhibitors?" Beck was holding up a white box reading from the label. In his other hand was the empty plastic bottle with a teaspoon of blood still in the bottom.

The cup of water stopped halfway to her lips. She obviously was surprised by this question. Franklin slowly blinked a few times. After a moment, she swished the water in her mouth before speaking.

"The CI variant of PVA is used in cryogenics to preserve organic matter. Are you saying…"

"Yes. I am." He set both items down on the counter. "There are about 2,000 of these bottles in the deep freeze. There's a machine just outside that deep freeze that's clearly labeled. It's designed to be so simple anyone can run it. It mixes the PVA into some solution with saline and then with the blood. It's automatically tested in a hematology analyzer and fast frozen."

"Looks like the ice cream machine at McDonald's where I worked in high school. But less complicated," Hodge added.

"Wait… How did you know it was safe for me to consume?"

"We tried it on Kepelos first. He was an asshole about it. He said it was delicious. He was surprised," Beck said. "He still doesn't know. Never will."

"He gets one daily as long as he keeps spilling his guts," Beck added.

"Don't trust that piece of shit," Franklin spat out.

"That's funny coming from you," Hodge replied.

"I've never killed anyone."

"And that's the only reason you're still alive," Beck said. "Your log said that if you get hungry enough, it becomes, and I quote, 'an all-consuming drive' that could eventually drive you insane or to murder."

Franklin turned her head away from them but nodded yes.

"Have you ever heard of Rhys Valmunin?" Beck asked.

"No. What's that?" Franklin said.

"Not a what, a who," Beck said as he began securing her bindings. "Kepelos tells quite a tale about him."

***

Valmunin lay back on his bed. Sikes rested on his chest. She seemed so tiny.

"I and my fellow Úlfhéðnar met her on one of the autumn raiding voyages," Valmunin said quietly. "We encountered a large trading vessel. It was a fine prize, and we took their ship and cargo without losing a single man. Their crew and passengers were killed to the last man, protecting a woman. Just this one woman."

"What is an Úlfhéðnar?" Sikes asked.

"Like a berserker, but better," he said, smiling.

"I just realized you only breathe when you speak," Sikes said. "Please go on."

"This was the very first Asian woman we'd ever seen. At first, because of her size, she was mistaken as a child until one of our crew tore her cloak away to reveal an exotic woman dressed in silk with long black hair."

Val slowly ran fingers down her spine as he continued.

"From the moment she was taken, I should've known something was wrong. This woman wouldn't have seen dawn any other time without being taken multiple times. Instead, dawn came, and a man was missing. The captain of the ship was named Ulf. He'd decided to take her as his share of the pillage. She slept all day below decks on the grand ship we had taken, and the captain stayed with her most of the time. Four more men disappeared in the month that followed as we headed for home. Usually, it was the night watch. No number of precautions stopped the people from vanishing. The crew blamed her, but Ulf wasn't to be crossed."

Sikes slid off his chest to his side, using his shoulder as a pillow.

"We were less than a day from home. We anchored in a cove at the mouth of the Isa Fjord. We always spent the last night out in this cove so that we'd arrive at the village midday. There would be a huge feast that night. Runes were carved in the rock walls surrounding the cove to ensure protection. They'd always worked... till that night."

"What happened?" Sikes now needed the rest of his story.

"I had taken to sleeping in the hold amongst the coils of rope, ax in hand, sitting up. I woke with a start, and she was standing before me. The bear fur from the captain's bed was wrapped around her slender shoulders. The fur fell away, and she stood there with her long black hair scattered across her body, wearing only a gold collar inscribed with runes. I didn't bother to read them."

"It was too late when I realized she'd already killed everyone on board, and the ship was on fire. I woke on the rocky beach, and she'd already drunk deeply from me... and I from her."

"Eventually, I realized she made me because she was afraid. She was a stranger in a strange land. She was lost, without the language, and in need of a protector. She taught me many things as we savagely made our way back to Japan. We were together almost 300 years."

He fell silent.

"You've killed lots of people?" It was more of a statement than a question. "Especially in the old days."

"Yes. I was a nightmare."

"Val, are you going to kill me?" Sikes asked outright.

"No... I'm not a savage anymore," he said, making eye contact with her. "Besides, I never play with my food..."

She punched his gut. Hard...

15. NO INNOCENT LIVES

"Valmunin started his crusade during the French Revolution." Kepelos started to spill again, desperate to cooperate. "He spent decades as a professional executioner before that. He met a French surgeon, Antoine Louis, who helped invent the guillotine." His words were spilling out fast now. "Everyone thought it was supposed to be more humane. It was just more efficient. Tidy. The blood was all collected in a vat below. And worse, they were better at killing vampires. The French aristocracy was filled with them. That's when he got a taste for the blood of his brothers."

"That was his source of blood?" Hodge asked

"When he saw one was a brother, he'd lift their head from the basket and look into their eyes. Tell them his name. He intended to drink their blood. He was the devil. A heretic."

"And it made him stronger?" Beck asked.

"More powerful, it gave him the voice, the power over lesser minds, and it also drove him mad in the gluttony of it. Soon, it was only the blood of brothers that could quench his thirst. And they finally subdued him, and he was laid upon his own guillotine."

"How did he escape?" Hodge asked.

"He didn't. The guillotine's blade shattered on his neck, and in a fury, he tore the entire thing apart with his bare hands. The legend says dozens of vampires had come to witness his death, and a battle ensued. The legend also says the Valkyries arrived and swept him away that day."

"Sounds like that grew in the telling," Hodge said.

"After that, his crusade began in earnest. He began hunting the brethren. He was good at it. He could use the Heretic power to make us do things, tell him things. The more brethren he'd consume, the greater his power. Humans were just food. He drove us to near extinction. Eventually, almost all the hunters in the world were gone. There was no one left to stand up to him. Large families, covens, packs, and nests were a thing of the past. He always found them. And killed them all."

"So, how did you survive for 202 years?" Hodge asked.

"I'm not a hunter," Kepelos confessed. "I'm a farmer."

***

"Where did Aiko go with the dogs?" Sikes asked after making love to him again. "Can you tell me?"

"She went to the Keep," he replied. "It's in the mountains, in Colorado."

"A Keep? That's what you call it? Sounds like a no-bullshit castle."

"Well, it's more like a monastery. It does have a huge tower, though, and a small cathedral. It's beautiful there," he said in a tone he knew would also convey the feeling.

"A cathedral? Won't you burst into flames or something if you go in there?" she teased.

"I've known many vampires that were priests. An entire coven of them were convinced that Jesus Christ himself was a vampire."

Sikes sat up, shock on her face.

"They were convinced that the blood of Christ ritual was based on actual events. His resurrection as well. They said he cured lepers with the blood of Christ, turning them. I'm not convinced. It makes you wonder, though."

"Wow, my mom would be screaming blasphemy. What else makes you wonder?" Sikes was curious now.

"Ever wonder why so many religions have a disdain for pigs?" Val asked.

"Because bacon is so good it's a sin?" Sikes quipped.

"We can survive on pig's blood," Val said. "Survive, but not thrive."

"That's some heavy heretic shit right there, man. Thanks for being honest about it. It's jacked up, but honest," Sikes said.

"While being honest, I need to tell you something. Something about you." Valmunin sat up, Indian style. Sikes mirrored him, looking amused. "I met you before, long ago."

"I would have remembered," she said.

"Not that night. You were too drunk, too busy destroying a bar full of rugby players."

"Jesus, you're talking about that night in Doubleday's in Rochester, New York. My guy had dumped me, I got drunk, got in a fight, got arrested, lost my wallet, and got eighteen stitches. I've no idea why they released me. I think I put twelve of those guys in the hospital. Don't get me wrong. Those asswipes deserved it."

"I know. I was there," Val said. "Let's just say you didn't put all twelve in the hospital."

"What? Why?" Sikes asked.

"I paid your bail, paid the damages to the bar. I had a chat with the asswipes, so they lied. They were too embarrassed to admit you kicked their asses. They said it was some bikers that busted them up," Val said. "So, they let you go."

"Why would you do all that?"

"I had been looking for you for over a century. Not you specifically. Someone like you."

"Wait… Things started to change for me after that. I kinda got my shit together. There were lucky breaks. When Master Takashi invited me to…gave me the job? It was not just a…"

"You're more than you know." Val held out a hand to her.

"What do you mean? More how? What am I?"

"A Valkyrie." He said, deep, low, and serious.

Her head tilted to the side as the thought sank in. She ignored his hand and climbed into his lap, wrapping her legs around his waist and arms around his neck.

"I've heard of Valkyries. Viking warriors, I think. Women, though," Sikes said, settling in.

"Valkyries are more than that. Their wills were made of steel," Valmunin whispered. "They do what they want. I hold no dominion over them, over you. Vampires cannot control them."

"We do what we want? Guess what I want…"

***

"Those were dark days," Kepelos continued. "There were no communications then. He'd decimate entire regions of brethren with a fury before moving on. Our culture was not organized. We were apex predators and only interacted with others of our kind when they trespassed on our territory. Only if one survived and fled did the tale spread at all. We were at the top of the food chain until then."

Beck had moved a chair into the infirmary to listen. Hodge had discovered a lab device designed to thaw and warm the bottles of blood and another to treat and quick-freeze the bottles. Kepelos hasn't noticed the difference. She brought him another pint, rewarding him and encouraging him to continue.

"It got worse," Kepelos went on. "He cultivated followers. A cult of human heretics." Kepelos was rolling. "He is why the word *cult* exists! Cult originally denoting homage paid to a divinity, from French culte or Latin cultus 'worship,' from cult—cultivated, worshipped! They thought he was a god. He used humans to train himself. He recruited the finest warriors. They followed him blindly because they believed him to be immortal. Legend says he'd generously reward any that could manage a killing blow. He'd been run through hundreds of times." Kepelos emptied the bottle through the straw this time, and his tone changed. "They became the hunters, and we the hunted. By the end of the American Civil War, the hunters had no prey left. Anywhere. Only those of us that hid deep survived."

"Why has he resurfaced now?" Beck asked.

"There were rumors that he went down with the Titanic. There was evidence it was true. But we still kept our heads down for another hundred years," Kepelos said. "This time, we had communications. We began a clandestine network. Created secret covens of the next generation with different rules. But the drive to be hunters was too much for some."

"But instead of Valmunin, humans began to hunt you," Beck said.

"Turns out humans were more aware than we thought. We thought it was him again. But it wasn't. It was the Catholic Church this time and not him at all. Until now."

***

"Tell me," Sikes said as she wrapped her legs around him, sitting in his lap, facing him.

"I had lost my way." Valmunin closed his eyes as he spoke, "During the French Revolution, I found an insatiable desire for the blood of my brethren. I had convinced myself that there was a path to redemption. As my power increased each time, I gorged myself on them. I foolishly thought it was a sign from the Gods. The Norse Gods. These Gods were not weak, or kind. I believed then that I had become a Draugar, an undead Víga-Hrappr. Perhaps I had."

"Go on."

"But I had been led by Shén Xiān and educated in the ways to care for myself. How to protect my eyes and skin from the sun. So, I never looked like a Víga-Hrappr with scarred, blackened skin or cloudy eyes."

"That's why you have the oil baths?"

"Yes. It's best if I look as human as possible," Val said.

"Just so you know, very few humans look like you."

***

"Tell me about others of your kind," Beck said. "Do you know a lot of other farmers? You said there was a network. Right now, that seems more important than Rhys Valmunin, who I presume is outside that network."

"It's organized in a way to keep everyone safe. Our locations secret. In case he… in case we… in case Valmunin found one of us. Found me. He couldn't torture information out of us we didn't know."

"So… you can't help us find more of your kind?" Beck stood up slowly.

Realization struck Kepelos slowly as Beck moved toward the door. When he turned off the light, the lab was absolutely dark.

"Wait!"

The panic echoed in the dark, but Beck didn't turn the light back on. His silhouette was outlined in the doorway.

"I know a place." There was horror in his voice. "But if I tell you and they find out… it would be far worse."

"Minus any additional information, all you're good for is experimentation. You can't imagine what that will be like." Beck didn't turn the lights back on. "You may have noticed the gaps in your restraints. Those gaps allow us to amputate your arms and legs. Then we'd remove your eyes. This reduces the likelihood of escape."

Kapelos began sobbing.

Beck decided to add a bluff. "Valmunin also recommends we remove the lower jaw after you've nothing left to tell us. Feeding tubes are easier then."

"His name is Aelfric Tauler. He's at least twice as old as me." It was coming out in a rush. "His farm is in the Catskills, but I send him cattle."

The lights came back on.

"And where exactly is this place?"

***

Beck entered the lab and turned on all the lights. It was instantly super bright, and Dr. Franklin closed her eyes tight. Hodge followed, carrying another bottle of blood. She set it down on a table and sat on a stool against the wall opposite where Franklin was bound. She had one of the KRISS carbines in her lap.

"Doctor, you're going to tell me everything you believe. I need to know," Beck said as he began to release the arm restraints. "I believe we have everything that Kapelos can tell us."

"Let me explain how this happened to me," Franklin began. "I was shocked to find the amount of research that had been done on a blood-based virus known simply as NS." She was nervously glancing at Hodge and the gun in her lap. "AIDS was, at first, considered to be a variation of this virus due to the fact that the virus was acquired by blood exchange and initial symptoms were very similar: drastic weight loss, weakness, vision anomalies, slowing metabolism, dramatic skin cancers." Beck removed the restraint from her head and arms. She scratched her nose and continued.

"Both viruses, in fact, attack the DNA directly. In the case of AIDS, the damage occurs in chromosomes that encode the replication of components required for the proper functioning of the immune system. NS also results in chromosome damage but in different areas and is a more difficult virus to transmit. Where a milliliter of blood will successfully transmit AIDS, as much as a liter is required to transmit NS."

"How would you transfer an entire liter of blood?" Hodge asked.

"An infusion needs far less. Drinking it, though, may need an entire liter. Less if the vampire is old."

Beck crossed his arms and waited for her to continue.

"Victims of NS don't test positive for HIV as people with AIDS do. Most die, misdiagnosed as having AIDS. The primary damage to the NS host DNA lies in these areas: the digestive tract, metabolism, circulatory systems, lymph systems, and cellular replication. Here is the frightening part." She paused. "NS stands for Nosferatu Syndrome."

"Instead of boring us with autopsy data and clinical technobabble, simply state the reality of it." Beck was getting impatient.

"The initial symptom of NS is the loss of involuntary control of the iris in the eye. The iris ultimately relaxes wide open, making direct sunlight extremely painful for the victim."

"Victim?" Hodge said.

"Gradually, most food is passed through the system undigested. Dramatic weight loss occurs. The skin becomes extremely susceptible to UV-catalyzed cancer, permanently driving the victim out of the sun."

Beck looked at Hodge.

"The only food source that would sustain an NS victim for any time was discovered to be pig's blood. The combinations of proteins, electrolytes, minerals, and salts were enough, barely enough. This is why it was called Nosferatu Syndrome in 1941."

"If a victim is correctly diagnosed and stabilized with proper diet, they can survive. Over several years, some dramatic changes occur: Metabolism slows the longer the patient lives; body temp drops, documented as low as 78F; body fat drops to less than 1%, causing eyes to look dark and sunken; the skin becomes paper-thin, very pale, almost transparent—the secretions from the stomach lining, liver and pancreas change chemically. The oddest symptom is that, over time, the victim accumulates iron in the skeletal tissue. All these symptoms are directly related to the diet."

"In one case, documented by the AMA, one victim, who after 15 years of barely surviving, began to have a dramatic turnaround in health. He had an amazing increase in muscle mass over a very short six-month period. Researchers were at a loss to determine why."

"There are photos of him included with the study. The subject's sex drive even returned, though he'd become sterile because of his limited diet. The iron content in his bones had gotten so high that he'd set off metal detectors in airports. He was the last known living NS subject."

"What happened to him?" Hodge asked.

"He disappeared. That was 1961. His name was Herold Page."

"What do you think happened?" Beck asked.

"I think he somehow started to drink human blood," Franklin said. "I think *all* the NS data was suppressed after that. People living with AIDS were already having a hard time in society. Imagine if the word got out that they might be vampires?"

16. THE CATSKILLS RAID

An unmarked, dark blue semi-truck and trailer stopped on the shoulder of I-88 just north of Richmondville, NY. It sat idling until a lone car passed.

The back door swung open in the darkness, and a flood of silent shadows spilled out. They were dressed from head to toe in black. Dozens of figures moved in unison across the dark open ground to the forest like a flock of swallows with one mind.

The only sound was the wind in the leaves.

***

"The dogs seem awful quiet tonight," one guard said to another as they strolled along the ten-foot-high chain link perimeter fence. "Where are they? They're usually attracted to the lights when we do a perimeter sweep."

The guards scanned the ten-yard space between the perimeter fences with their flashlights.

"Don't get too close to the fence. You might set off the metal detectors in the dog run again. I don't want to explain that... again." They backed away from the fence a few paces but kept walking.

One guard scanned his light up to the razor wire that topped the fence.

"What do you think the dogs are up to? And where?"

"Shut the fuck up. Something's not right here." That guard's tactical light came on. It was mounted to a rail on his M4 carbine.

His light froze on two sleeping dogs lying down by the outer fence.

The simultaneous blows of the butt end of a well-used red oak staffs put them face down in the fresh-cut grass. They were quickly stripped of weapons and radios. Their hands were cuffed behind their back with the handcuffs from their own belts. Their ankles were bound together with heavy zip ties. Last, they were bound to each other at hands and feet. The tactical lights switched off.

It all took less than 30 seconds.

It was happening all around the perimeter.

***

"No, it doesn't harm the dogs," Valmunin said as he activated the plastic ball and tossed it over the fences to the left and right of the gate. "These smell like rotting meat and will attract the dogs but will not set them off. They're trained not to eat food if you toss it in. So they can't be poisoned. But they'll sniff things. And sniffing will give them a nice dose of sleeping gas. It wears off in about six hours."

They watched all four dogs lie down for nap time.

"Now we wait," he said, but they didn't have to wait long. A shadowy figure approached the fence at the edge of the pool of light over the gate. Valmunin flashed a light, and a moment later, a hand-held radio seemed to fall from the sky, trailing a black silk scarf.

Valmunin caught it easily.

"What's with the scarf?" Sikes asked as the shadow disappeared.

"It slows the flight and makes a sound as it falls. Easier to catch," Valmunin said as he turned up the volume slightly on the radio. "We can't cross, or the entire compound will go on lockdown. It has ground-based metal detectors. Waiting for me. It's why Takashi and crew carry no weapons but wooden staffs. No gear but plastic zip ties."

Ten minutes later, the radio chimed in.

"Sector one. Check-in." There was a pause of thirty seconds. "Sector one, radio check... Sector two, radio check." There was another 30-second pause. "Dave, I think comms are down. Do you read?"

"I hear you, Sanders. All personnel, please radio check."

"Red post one check."

"Red post two check."

"West post check."

There was a pause.

"East post? South?" Pause. "Red post two, walk around to East post... Red Post two?"

An audible alarm sounded in the distance.

"Time to go," Valmunin said, tearing the chain link fence open like paper. Stepping past the sleeping dogs, another alarm sounded as he tore the inner fence open. Floodlights came on everywhere.

Just inside, a golf cart pulled out from behind the adjacent guard shack. Master Takashi pulled up with a smile, and they climbed in.

It was a winding half mile to the rustic lodge. All the floodlights were on now. At least twenty of Valmunin's men surrounded each door. Half of them were now armed with confiscated M4s.

The two guards that had been posted at the front door were gone. Much to Valmunin's surprise, the front door was not locked.

Four of Val's men dragged a heavily bound man up the steps to face him.

"What are we facing here?" Valmunin's eyes were glowing now. Something in the sound of his voice compelled the man to speak the instant the question was asked.

"None of us are ever allowed inside the residence. House staff only."

Val gestured the man away. An instant later, he was unconscious and face down in the grass by two others.

"Stay sharp" was all Val said. Sikes was directly behind him. A hooded group carrying M4s flooded into the Lodge behind him. They moved in every direction, clearing the house.

The Lodge was massive—room after room of opulence. One high-ceiling room was full of massive big game trophies and weapons mounted on the wall.

Sikes was drawn to a wall of swords. From the center, she drew down a beautiful katana.

Her smile would have unnerved an average person.

Rounding another corner, there was a man standing there as if patiently waiting. He looked like a traditional, well-trained, old-school butler. The neatly groomed white hair, goatee beard, and single raised eyebrow.

"Right this way, sir." He made a subtle bow and gestured to the open door he stood next to.

Val paused in front of him. "What's your name?"

"My name is Daniel, sir," he replied.

"Take me to the master of the house." His voice carried weight. The commands were as irresistible as gravity.

"Very good, sir."

They proceeded down panel-lined halls. They were crowded with fine paintings. At last, they entered a sparsely furnished drawing room. A large fire roared in an enormous fireplace. In the center of the room stood a vampire holding a Falcata sword.

"I'm Page, and you probably don't remember me. But I remember you…"

Valmunin ignored him. The perfect insult.

"Daniel, the Master. Please."

Page roared as he attacked.

***

Sikes somehow knew that Valmunin was leaving this one to her. When Page roared in rage and advanced to attack Valmunin, he hadn't even noticed her yet.

She easily parried the blow as it descended toward Val's neck. And with an additional twist and flick, she sent all four of Page's sword-hand fingers flying.

His sword clattered to the floor as he stared at her in disbelief.

As Daniel led Valmunin out a door at the opposite end, Sikes spoke. "Pick it up," she said, "Just taking your head would be no fun at all." To add insult to injury, she transferred her katana to her left hand.

"You fucking bitch." Page retrieved the sword and instantly attacked with a flurry of strikes. All were impossibly parried, and the last strike was overpowered in his rage, and as he passed her, she sliced deep into the back of one of his thighs.

"Who the fuck are you?"

"Nobody, really. My name's Pam. He leaves the easy ones to me. He gets bored. Has lots of more important things to do today." She deflected another series of enraged attacks but gave no ground doing so.

"How did you get past the guards?" Page evidently thought talking would distract her. "There are over a hundred out there."

"Bored and distracted humans. Reliant on tech." She walked away from him, showing him her back. "Metal detectors? No motion sensors? As if all you were afraid of was him. I guess your dogs and dumbass guards would just set them off constantly."

There was automatic gunfire briefly from within the building elsewhere, close enough that it made her glance at the door she came in. She barely dodged in time.

His sword bit into her flesh just above her right knee.

"Enough playing," Page pronounced just before his head came off his neck.

"Fuck." She kicked Page's severed head like a soccer ball, sending it into the fireplace. "Goal!" Page's face looked out as the coals set his hair on fire.

Sikes cut a pant leg off Page's body and bandaged her wound.

She followed the direction Daniel had taken Val.

***

Daniel led him down a much narrower hallway to stairs that descended a level. Val left all the doors open behind him.

The last door was already open and led to what seemed to be a large butler's pantry. A large open trapdoor was in the center of the floor at the far end.

"Sir, it is likely a trap. I've the sense that Lord Tauler expected you at some point." Daniel lowered his eyes. "Will you kill me now? I believe I may deserve it. There's always been much evil in this house."

"Will you retire? Try to make amends?" Val asked, using his power, his voice, to cement the notion.

"Yes, sir."

"We will be gone from here in less than an hour. I know the security detail outside had no idea what was happening in here. Help them after we are gone."

"And the others, sir?" He pointed down the stone spiral stairs.

Val just nodded.

The stairs descended at least fifty feet and opened into what looked like a well-kept medical clinic. There was a long, dimly lit, clean hallway with black painted walls. Twelve wide hallways labeled A through L branched off to the left at regular intervals. Each was a dead end.

The halls were lined with cells separated by thick cement walls. Valmunin presumed that the thick, floor-to-ceiling glass was a one-way mirror. Each cell held one prisoner. Most sat in overstuffed chairs, eating and watching TV. The TV was massive and mounted behind mirrored glass on the far wall.

Only the chair and sleeping platform were in the room. Both were part of the floor.

There were forty cells in each hall. Twenty on each side. It was mostly women and slightly obese men. In two cells, men were showering just beyond the glass. The next cell down the hall turned on when their shower turned off. The occupants disrobed and placed their clothes in a steel hatch at the far end. They began their showers.

Walking back, he now noticed confusion with some prisoners. They sat on their towel and watched TV. Some kept opening the cupboard only to find the crumpled sweats they just put in there.

Valmunin noticed doors in the middle of each wall segment in the main corridor. It was a maintenance hall on the TV side of the cell rows. These provided access to the hatches into each cell.

Behind the second one, he found a freshly dead body. There was a bullet hole in the Hispanic woman's head. He searched each corridor, and the maintenance access corridors.

In the last cell of Row L, on the outer wall, was Tauler. He was sitting on the edge of the bed with a remote control in his wrinkled hand.

The glass was different here. It was instantly obvious that Tauler could see Val as well as he could see Tauler. He pressed a button on the remote, and his voice flowed from a hidden speaker above.

"You got past Page faster than I thought you would," Tauler began but flinched when Valmunin struck the center of the glass panel with a massive blow from a hammer fist.

The glass held.

"I've been watching you. Ever since the French Revolution, actually." He stood and approached the glass as he spoke. "I had a plan to help you escape and join my coven. But that all went sideways."

His skin was so wrinkled, dry, and cracked it almost looked burned. Only a few wisps of hair remained.

"I placed a lead link in the chain that bound you to the stone stake. The alchemist brew they used to capture you wore off in time. Alas, no rescue from the flames for your beloved Asian friend."

"It was your kind that authored our capture. The alchemist, priest, and mayor all paid in the end," Valmunin growled. "Who were you? A minor minion I didn't notice?"

"What are you doing, Valmunin?" Tauler said with a change in tone. "You've seen the cattle here. They're well cared for and well fed. Entertained. They enjoy better lives here than out there." He pointed a bony finger up. They're sedated, and blood is extracted once every two months. They don't even know it's happened. "They're fat and happy."

"I'm not here for them," Val growled.

"They're cattle. Well-cared-for cattle. You do the same thing. But your cattle think they give you their blood freely. We are the same. I just don't bother to brainwash them."

"And now you share a cage with your cattle."

"Oh, this isn't a cage. It's a trap for you, my naïve friend. While I stalled with conversation, the lodge was in full flames by now. Pressing the final button will flood the sprinklers above you and in the cells with gasoline and then flame. Goodbye, my friend. You were a worthy tool."

Tauler pressed a button, and the wall behind him slid aside.

***

The katana came down so fast it was invisible.

The arm holding the remote fell to the floor, severed cleanly at the elbow. Before the limb touched the floor, the blade opened his throat all the way to the spine. It was stopped only by the iron vertebra.

She was relentless—chops to the left of the neck and then to the right. A defensive wound severed Tauler's other hand. Hamstrings and Achilles tendons were sliced in a dance, circling this thing that wouldn't die. Chunks of flesh flew in every direction as if she were determined to carve him down to bones.

Tauler had collapsed to the floor. He could no longer support the iron skeleton. His back was arched over the end of the bed. His jaw wide open, his ears and cheeks were gone.

A strong hand stopped the next blow from behind.

It was Valmunin. His touch had stopped Sikes's berserker rage.

He pried the katana from her hands. He examined the ruined blade briefly. Then, looking into Tauler's eyes, he said, "Fool."

With a precise, powerful blow, the blade found the minute space between his vertebra and severed his head. Valmunin left the ruined katana embedded into the platform and kicked the head into the hallway beyond.

Sikes stood in the doorway, breathing hard next to Daniel.

Unshaken, he retrieved the remote control before speaking, "We will have to hurry, sir." He pressed a button on the remote, and behind them, another panel slid aside, revealing a long wide corridor.

There was a large golf cart parked there.

"This way, sir," Daniel said with his usual gesture.

"What about them?" Sikes pointed to the other cells.

Daniel pressed another button and all the cell doors opened, revealing the access corridors. "They'll find their way out behind us. We shall leave all the doors open. The authorities will find them."

They piled into the golf cart and quickly drove at least a mile to emerge into the forest in a small clearing that held a private helicopter.

Sikes and Valmunin climbed out of the cart, but Daniel remained.

"You can come with us. We owe you that," Sikes said.

"No. The security detail is innocent as well. I will go back and free them. Any story they present will be more plausible than the truth."

"Thank you, Daniel," Valmunin said.

Daniel only nodded and drove away down a path through the woods.

"Can you fly a helicopter?" Valmunin asked.

"What? No!" Sikes replied.

"It's a good thing I can…"

17. THE SILO

"Do you know why vampires hate water?" Beck asked Franklin. "It's because they lose the ability to swim. Low body fat combined with iron in their bones makes them sink like a stone. Sure, they can survive under there for a long time. But drowning is certain after a long enough period. Remember stories of witch hunters and their dunking stools to test for witches? They'd bind them to a chair and lower them under water for fifteen minutes or more. If you lived, you were deemed a witch and burned at the stake. If you died, well, you went to heaven instead."

"Why tell me this?" Franklin asked.

"Because you're in the middle of the ocean. Hundreds of miles from anywhere. Outside normal shipping lanes, on a fixed platform oil rig. The water here is a shallow 600 feet deep. Do you have any feeling of hydrophobia yet?" Beck asked.

"Like the rabies symptom?"

"Yes, exactly like the rabies symptom. Another similar blood-based transmitted virus."

"I… I don't know."

***

"I always wanted a Bell 429 helicopter. I never got around to it," Valmunin said as they climbed in. On the outside, it was all forest camouflage. Sitting in this tall grass, seeing from above, would be very difficult. It was all luxury leather and wood panels inside.

"When and why the hell did you learn to fly a helicopter?" Sikes asked, and the engine spun to life, and Valmunin handed her a headset.

"I was a chopper pilot in Vietnam. I used to follow wars for what I hope are obvious reasons. The last time I was shot down was quite a long walk home."

After a few minutes, the chopper softly lifted into the air. They circled the Lodge, which was now fully engulfed in flames. Some of the guards had been freed and were helping other guards move away from the inferno.

Valmunin turned to follow the highway and soon found the familiar tractor-trailer moving back toward the city.

"Why are you flying so low? You don't need to impress me," Sikes said.

"Air space in this region is tightly controlled—no flight plan. No transponder. Plus, there are no registration numbers visible that I could see. So we will fly low and quiet."

The flight from the Catskills to the city was uneventful and quiet at 3:30 a.m. When they approached the warehouse, it was in flames.

"What happened?" Sikes asked.

Valmunin didn't respond. Instead, he turned and flew low over the Hudson River.

"Where are we going?"

"Hoboken" was all he said. Soon followed by, "That mother fucker."

There was another fire. Half a block of brownstones were ablaze.

He kept flying low over the water. The sun was beginning to rise when he began to hover over a pier in a deserted section of Port Socony Reach. A barge was burning below. There were no emergency vehicles around this one.

"I'm not as smart as I thought," Valmunin said. "I've been a fool."

"What were those places?" Sikes asked.

"Safehouses. Secondary safehouses. All of them."

The chopper took a hard turn and was quickly out over the open water. The shore was shrinking behind them.

"Where are we going now?" Sikes asked.

"I know a safe place where we can think."

***

Hodge and Beck explored and searched the facility. It was far more extensive than they first assumed. A server room had several consoles logged on that monitored the facility and its water, power, comms, solar, and security.

"A natural gas well powers the primary and secondary generators when required. The solar seems to handle most of the current power demands," Hodge said as she tabbed through the screens. "I think someone has been here more often than we were led to believe."

She was clicking through windows rapidly when Beck noticed something. "Hang on. Go back. That security screen. On the right there." He pointed to a date time-stamped log arranged by dates, calendar style. The entry for today said 113. Drilling down, they could see themselves starting on the helipad and sitting there in the server room.

Without prompting, she began to page back. She stopped three months earlier. 390 and 228 were listed on a few dates in August.

Drilling in, they saw two people climbing out of a chopper. First, it was the pilot, Oddjob.

Then, it was Daniel Rawn, also known as Switch.

"They split up as soon as they arrived and stayed overnight," Hodge said. "Without watching all 96 hours of footage, it looks like Oddjob is doing maintenance on stuff. Checking oil in the generators, dusting debris off the solar panels, changing water filters."

"What's Switch doing?" Beck asked.

"He seems to be sitting at a terminal drinking coffee. The whole time." She pointed to a vid of a rec room. The view shows Switch beyond a ping-pong table and a pool table. He was sitting at a computer at the far end of the room.

"He even sleeps on that couch and comes right back to it," Hodge says.

"Can this system show us what he was working on?" Beck asked.

"No. But if we go down there, we might learn something." Hodge got up.

It took longer than expected to find the rec room. This room had windows on two walls and included a balcony. Beck opened the sliding glass door to let in some fresh air to the stuffy room that still smelled of cigarettes and stale beer. The computer was powered up already. The desktop was filled with dozens of computer game icons.

"Don't tell me he was just playing computer games," Beck said.

"This computer somehow has access to the internet," Hodge said as she brought up the browser history. "Looks like he was looking for something in Google Maps—lots of real estate sites. Wholesale suppliers. All in North Dakota."

"Are there any recent documents saved on here around that date?"

She did a date-based search and found a folder of files saved on that day.

"Most of these are screencaps from Google Maps," Hodge said.

"Why are all these blurred out?" Beck asked. "Why bother? Looks like abandoned…" Beck stopped mid-sentence.

"There's a way you can request they do that."

"Open that one." Beck pointed with his finger.

It was a screencap from archive.org, the Internet Wayback Machine.

It was a real estate listing for a decommissioned Titan Missile silo.

"Look, this is a flight and car rental confirmations to Bismarck, North Dakota. Leaving from Buffalo, New York, with a layover in Chicago," Hodge said.

"Wasn't he killed on his way to Chicago?"

Both their heads turned toward the open door to the balcony at the same time.

They could hear a chopper approaching.

18. LIES REVEALED

The helicopter was already set down when Beck and Hodge retrieved their weapons and found their way back to the right helipad.

As their heads cleared the deck, they saw two people waiting for them as the blades spun down.

"You?" Beck said. He recognized the vampire. "How did you find me?"

Freya rushed up to the vampire and sat with her tail wagging rapidly. A small hand gesture, and she lay down at his feet, unmoving.

"I didn't expect to find you here," the vampire said coolly. "Much has happened. We should talk."

"You knew Switch?" Beck said, unable to hide the confusion on his face. "Let's go inside."

Beck turned his back to them and descended the stairs. He knew if the vampire wanted him dead, he'd be dead already. He paused before opening the door. They waited at the top of the stairs as Hodge descended them backward with her carbine still trained on them.

"Get a thawed bottle from the fridge in the lab," Beck said quietly in her ear as she passed him into the corridor. Beck walked down the corridor and paused by the double doors that led into the mess hall. Then he entered the hall and sat at a table close to the counter.

Valmunin and Sikes cautiously entered and came to sit at the table. Before Beck could speak, Hodge entered. As she walked to the table, Beck said, "Are you hungry? We've some chili-mac on the stove."

His tone was casual. Hodge set the bottle on the table in front of Valmunin and sat on the opposite side next to Beck. Both her hands were again on the carbine.

"Please forgive me," Beck began again. "I'm Timothy Beck, and this is my associate, Maris Hodge." He gestured to Valmunin, "As you may remember, we met you briefly on a prior occasion…"

"Hi, I'm Pam Sikes, and to be honest, I've had a long fucking day, and chili-mac sounds kinda awesome at this moment." She stood and followed her nose through the gap in the long counter into the kitchen beyond.

Hodge followed her.

"I know Switch is dead," Valmunin said, then drew a deep breath through his nose.

"Yes. I'm his replacement."

"Switch was a good man. A difficult man to replace," Valmunin said.

"I've heard much about you since we last met. Are you saying you didn't kill him?"

"He was my friend. I've had precious few over the centuries," Valmunin said, sadness slipping into his tone.

"What are you doing here?" Beck asked.

"I was about to ask you the same thing," Valmunin said.

There was a long pause. Neither continued.

***

Sikes and Hodge found a pot of chili on the stove. In a warming oven was a casserole dish of mac and cheese. Hodge handed over two bowls and said, "You ever wonder how we got involved in this insanity?"

"To be honest, I haven't had time to wonder," Sikes said as she spooned a heaping helping of mac and cheese, followed by an equal helping of chili on top. "Last week, I was just the ice delivery guy."

"Ahhh… no beans," Hodge said. "Real chili."

"Girl after my own heart," Sikes said. "What about what's his face?" She gestured with a half-empty bowl.

"Yeah. Why not." Hodge said as she opened the fridge nearby. "Rolling Rock, OK?"

"I hope we don't start trying to kill each other. I kinda love you guys already." Sikes set down the bowls and expertly opened one green, non-twist-off bottle on the counter's edge. She took a long pull, draining half the bottle.

Hodge similarly opened two other bottles. "You kinda got stuff splattered on you." She pointed at Sikes's clothes. You can wash up there if you want." She pointed to the large industrial sink.

Sikes noticed the back of her hand as she was about to have another drink from the long-neck bottle.

"Oh shit. Sorry," Sikes said in earnest.

"Grab one of the small towels. It's kinda on the right side of your face, too," Hodge pointed.

"Dammit."

Sikes spent a minute scrubbing her face and hands. Standing up and facing Hodge, she asked, "How's that?"

Hodge took the wet towel from her, scrubbed a final spot behind her ear, and dropped the towel in the sink.

"Valmunin's not going to kill you," Sikes said. "Maybe the vampires that are here. But not you two. He would have already."

"How does he know there are vampires here?" Hodge asked as she placed a spoon in each of the two bowls she had there and carried a beer and a bowl in each hand back toward the mess hall.

"He can smell them. He pretends it's a sigh. But he breathes them in."

***

Valmunin took the glass stopper off the top of the liter-sized bottle and lifted it for a sniff. Without a word, he drained the bottle without swallowing.

"I helped Switch develop this." He looked at the bottle as if it might speak. "It seems he got it right."

"Why didn't the team know about this? About you?" Beck asked.

"He believed the team was compromised."

"He was right. One of them was a vampire. She's in restraints in one of the labs."

"And who's the other vampire? That one is much older."

"His name is Kapelos. We are questioning him," Beck said, causing an eyebrow to react on Valmunin's face.

Just then, Hodge returned with food. She set a bowl and a beer in front of him. Sikes set her own bowl down in her seat across from them. She dropped a handful of white washcloths on the center of the table.

"They don't believe in paper towels around here, so these will have to do as napkins," Sikes said, barely before the first of many hungry mouthfuls silenced her.

"They minimize trash, maximize reuse," Beck said.

"What did you just say?" Hodge asked.

"Paper towels. Single-use trash. This they can launder several hundred times."

"Maximize reuse..." Hodge trailed off, eating, thinking.

"Did Kapelos tell you about the Lodge yet?" Valmunin asked.

"He did. And I've no idea why I'm telling you this," Beck said as he ate. "We were about to call for pickup to inform Sloan about it when you showed up. It's probably our next mission."

"No. I don't think so," Valmunin said flatly, but his tone conveyed absolute certainty. "We just came from there."

"And Tauler?" Beck asked.

"That's him spattered all over Sikes," Valmunin said.

"Jesus, Val. I washed up!" Sikes looked at her jeans.

"Reuse..." Hodge said absently again. "Do you know anything about a Titan missile silo north of Bismarck, North Dakota?"

"No. But let's go see if your other guests might." Valmunin stood.

"Dr. Franklin won't know anything about it. Kapelos might," Beck said.

"Franklin?" Valmunin stopped in his tracks. His head turned back toward them. "Franklin is a vampire?"

"Yes. She confessed. Told us the whole story, and I believe her," Beck said.

Two minutes later, they entered the lab where Franklin was being held. She was restrained at the opposite end of the room and squeezed her eyes shut when the bright overhead lights came on. Beck used the dimmer to lower them a bit before he walked to the far side of the gurney she was bound to.

At the sound of footsteps, she turned and saw Valmunin slowly crossing the room toward her. His eyes were glowing from some internal fire. Beck had the sense that he was moving in slow motion. He felt a kind of incomplete paralysis. If he had to move, it would be like swimming in thick, invisible honey that was laced with menace.

All of it was directed at Franklin.

When he reached the foot of her gurney, he stopped and focused directly on her. Her eyes were wide, and her mouth was open in a silent scream.

Franklin peed herself.

Just then, they heard the explosion.

***

"Sir, may I speak with you? Privately," Oddjob asked Sloan as he walked across the hangar from the command trailer to his RV.

Oddjob took off his headset and set his smartphone on the conference table. Sloan took the hint and did the same.

They left the main hangar door and began walking to the refueling stations.

"What's this about?" Sloan was always direct with Oddjob.

"I received this from a confidential informant." Oddjob handed him an old-style flip phone. It was not a smartphone, but it did accept text messages. There was a single text message.

The nest is still burning.

The text concluded with Lat/Long coordinates.

"Get Gram and Tank. We dust off in five minutes. FBI/SIU ident badges. I'll get Snow." Sloan began to move.

"Sir, I recommend we roll radio silent starting now." Oddjob didn't wait for an acknowledgment.

They were in the air in four minutes. It took nearly two hours before they saw the thick plume of black smoke. They circled a few times before landing upwind from the smoke inside the compound's perimeter. There were dozens of emergency vehicles, and even a medical triage and a command tent were set up.

Sloan quickly found out the local sheriff named Rhonda Garrett was in charge at the site. As he approached her, Sloan had seen the look on her face many times on others in the past. He moved directly to defuse potential problems.

"Sheriff Garrett, my name is John Miller with the Special Investigation Unit at the FBI," Sloan lied, extending a hand to shake and producing a business card. His badge hung around his neck from a black lanyard. "I'm not here to take over your investigation. I may, in fact, be able to help."

Garrett was a dark-skinned black woman with a short haircut that was nearly a buzz cut. She had deep lines on her face. Her sheriff's uniform was pristine.

"What is it you're investigating, Mr. Miller?" Garrett asked. Sloan had seen the five school buses parked on the site and others on the way during the flight.

"We are investigating human trafficking of homeless people taken from the streets in various large cities," Sloan said.

"Well, you've come to the right place." Garrett gestured to the large emergency medical tent. "We have 466 victims, but none of them seem to know anything. None seem to have been abused beyond their confinement. More than half are illegal immigrants. Most were taken from New York City and the surrounding area."

"What about those three there?" Sloan pointed to three men dressed in black BDUs sitting on the ground, surrounded by deputies who were keeping an eye on them.

"We also found seven security guards that were un-conscious and bound with their own cuffs. Three of them are awake but not talking. The other four have been rushed to the hospital."

"I don't want to take too much of your valuable time. Our field office can get copies as long as your reports make it to NYPD. No special actions are required on your part."

"What were they doing with these people?" Garrett asked sincerely. "They didn't even know there were other people here."

"We believe the traffickers kidnap them from the streets and restore their health," Sloan said. "And then they… They catalog their blood types and genomes into an international organ-harvesting black market database. Have your medical team look for kidney harvesting scars."

Garrett's face was horrified. The lie made sense.

"Can I talk to one or two of the victims? Are there any that are better witnesses? Communicators," Sloan asked.

"Yes. I think I know just the one." Garrett led the way out of the command tent. They began to walk across the field to the medical tent.

"What time did you arrive here? It's just now 1100," Sloan asked.

"Fire and rescue were called in just before dawn. The blaze could be seen from miles away. I got here about an hour ago from Kingston. The fire investigators had already called it. Arson. Gasoline all throughout. They'd seen it before. Classic evidence destruction."

They walked toward the first school bus.

"How long have you been county sheriff?" Sloan asked.

"Eleven years. So far," she said. "Wait here."

Sloan waited a half a dozen paces from the bus. He scanned the area, noticing Tank was speaking to the deputies watching the security men. Snow nodded as she slipped out of the medical tent and headed back to the chopper.

***

The explosion rocked glassware from the wall shelves that divided the labs. They rushed to the hallway to find the next door hanging from the bottom hinge.

What was left of Kapelos was just inside the door. He'd somehow escaped the restraints that Houdini couldn't. A glance at the gurney told the story. His left arm was still in the restraint. He was able to rip his own arm off at the shoulder socket, allowing him to slide his right arm out.

"Maybe we should have mentioned the collar," Hodge said.

Valmunin found the head. He lifted it by the hair and looked into its eyes. They were still moving. While holding it in one hand, he lifted the headless body with the other, placing it on an autopsy table. Thick fluid began to run out of the corpse into a drain and a basin below.

He propped the head so it could watch its life drain away in its final minutes.

"Kapelos, I will drink your blood and that of your master."

"That's harsh, dude," Sikes said from the doorway.

Beck and Hodge looked over their shoulders at her.

"What?" Sikes said.

***

"Agent Miller, this is Kelly Lopez. Kelly helped lead everyone out and kept them calm before we arrived. Kelly is atypical in this group. She was not homeless. She was a student at Essex County College."

She nodded but said nothing.

"Kelly, can you briefly tell me what happened to you? Not just today. From the beginning of it."

"It's my fault. I was walking home from a party…" She faltered.

"It's OK. No judgment here," Sloan reassured her.

"I threw up, and I guess I passed out in an alley." She looked up at Sloan as she gathered strength. "I woke up locked in a shipping container. In the dark. The only light was from a slot cut on the floor."

"The slot was just big enough to slide in a pizza every couple days?" Sloan said. "A five-gallon bucket and a thin mattress on the floor?"

"Yes… exactly." She was trying not to cry.

"How long were you there?" Sloan asked.

"There were six pizzas. No days. No time in the dark."

"Then you woke up here?"

"Yes. I expected horrors in the dark. In my own filth. It was hell. This place was a relief by comparison. The hot, delicious meals every day, clean clothes, showers daily, even TV and music. But it was still a prison… I never saw or spoke to another person—no other inmates. I thought I was alone. And no jailer."

"What else can you tell me?" Sloan asked gently.

"I thought aliens had kidnapped me. I'm serious. I was in the Medical preparatory program at Essex. I know what an IV bruise looks like. Every couple of months, I'd wake up with needle marks. No memory of anything happening. I was sure it was aliens."

"How did you get your meals?" Garrett asked.

"They had, like, a dumbwaiter. Do you know what a dumbwaiter is? The door would slide up. Food was there. Put your dishes in it when you were done, and it took them away.

If you didn't, no more food. A new sweat suit shows up, put the old set in, or no food either." She was rolling now. "After a couple months, I woke up, and my hair was gone—Buzz cut. Nothing could get a reaction. Not screaming and not trashing your cell, not shredding your clothes, sheets, blankets, or pillow. They didn't give a fuck. So, I gave up. I ate. I watched TV and slept a lot. Almost three years." Tears were coming back.

Garrett pulled out her cell phone. "We were going to handle this back in Kingston, but is there anyone we can call?" She held out the phone.

Kelly choked out, "My mom…" She took the phone and dialed the number from memory but handed the phone back to Garrett as it began to ring. Kelly buried her face in her hands and started to sob.

Sloan squeezed her shoulder and said, "Thank you." He was surprised. She hugged Sloan around the middle, burying her face in his ribs.

"Mrs. Lopez, my name is Rhonda Garrett. We found your daughter safe and sound. She's right here. One moment." She handed the phone to Kelly.

"Momma… I'm all right. I'm so sorry, momma…"

Sloan was walking back to the chopper. Garrett was following and stopped him after enough distance to give Kelly space.

"So, you know more about this than I need to know," Garrett began. "I will file a detailed report, but it sounds like you're already on top of it. It's a sleepy county, Agent Miller. I can see why they chose it."

"We raided the supplier with the shipping containers a few days ago. Don't be surprised if you get nothing from those guards, either. I'd wage a million dollars that they're contract workers with no idea what was happening here. Besides, they're all trained to lawyer up fast and keep their mouths shut."

"Yes. I can see that," she said.

"Just make sure their names and company names are in the report. That may be helpful," Sloan said, reaching out his hand to shake.

"I'm glad there were no children," Garret said out of the blue.

"Try not to wonder why too much," Sloan said, turning away.

The rotors were spinning up before he reached the chopper. Once everyone was inside with headsets on, they were in the air.

"It was another farm. Kapelos was the supplier," Sloan said as they circled the site two more times.

"I gotta say, boss, this has the smell of Beck and Hodge all over it," Tank said. "Have they checked in?"

"No. They haven't. Dammit." Sloan added nothing more. He was looking at Snow. He was sure she knew more than she told him, just like Oddjob.

Two hours later, Snow set the chopper down directly in front of the open hangar.

Beck and Hodge sat relaxing on folding chairs in the shade of the building, petting the dog that sat pretty between them. They looked relaxed even though the black carbines rested in their laps.

When the helicopter doors opened, they stood, moved to the center of the wide hangar door, and waited for them. Snow remained in the chopper, performing shutdown procedures. Gram and Tank flanked Sloan with their heavy rigs in low ready.

"Can we take this reunion inside so we are a bit less conspicuous?" Sloan asked.

"Can we call the entire team to the command trailer? We need to show you something," Beck said. "Easier to tell everyone at once."

Tank and Gram went to wake the third-shift members who were sleeping. Sloan entered the command trailer to find it empty.

"Where the fuck is Coffee? He knows better than to leave the comms unmanned," Sloan cursed.

"He'll be here in a second," Beck said as the last of the team crowded in. He made a gesture to the dog. Palm up closed into a fist and then rolled over. Freya immediately got up and worked her way through the whole team, sniffing them as she went. She worked her way all the way to the back and forward again.

Everyone remained silent.

"We've been compromised. Switch found this out and died before he could act," Beck began, to a silent room. "Coffee is a vampire. A Stage Two at least."

"We scanned him. He was clean," Sloan replied.

"Why do you think he drank so much coffee? It kept his core temp up. But core temp couldn't fool Freya," Beck said as he nodded to Hodge, who knocked twice on Sloan's office door at the front of the trailer.

The door opened, and Coffee emerged. He didn't walk. He seemed to float, carried by a single hand around his neck. His shirt was shredded. Both his shoulders were obviously dislocated, and his arms were cruelly tied behind his back. They touched from his elbows to his wrists, bound with some kind of steel cable, wrapped over and over.

None of them seemed to notice Valmunin was holding him up by the neck.

Then the veil of stupor seemed to lift, and they all saw him as well as the blond woman at his elbow. They all instantly drew weapons and aimed at Valmunin.

No one fired.

"Please don't shoot him. It might piss him off." The blond woman said casually.

"Chief, I'd like to introduce Pam Sikes, and this is Rhys Valmunin. The oldest vampire in the world. He was friends with Switch and has been hunting vampires for centuries."

Sloan holstered his Glock and motioned for everyone else to do the same. "Beeker, please help our guest secure Coffee in the med bay—the usual protocol. Then let's all convene at the conference table. The pizza will be here soon."

Sloan shook his head as he exited the command trailer and walked to the open hangar doors alone to await the pizza guy.

"We called the order in from the chopper. It's almost 2 o'clock. No breakfast, no lunch," Snow said.

They all watched Beeker lead them into the lab trailer.

"Pizza sounds good right now," Sikes said to Hodge.

They were all staring at her now.

"Oh… it gets better. Trust me." Sikes said, looking around the hangar. "Your fucked-up-scale-o-meters don't go high enough."

Sloan soon returned with a dozen large pizzas and spread them across the conference table.

Everyone stood while they ate pizza in silence.

Chen started to ask a question, but Sloan held up a hand, and he fell silent.

Finally, when Beeker joined them, looking over his shoulder to discover the vampire was not there, Sloan sat and spoke.

"Beck, did you destroy the compound in the Catskills?" Sloan asked, getting directly to the point.

Sikes answered through a mouthful of pizza. "No. That was us." She was pointing between the lab and herself rapidly.

Sloan just waited.

"Here is the short version. We were interrogating Franklin and Kapelos when Valmunin and Sikes showed up," Beck said. "By the time we found out about the Lodge from Kapelos, it was already destroyed. The thing is, Switch had already been working with Valmunin. The katana we found in the cab belonged to Switch." Beck had a long look at Oddjob but didn't mention him, giving him a chance to speak.

Oddjob was stoic. He said nothing.

"I think Switch had uncovered the Lodge," Beck continued but looked at Sikes now. She was still eating pizza.

"Don't look at me. I don't know shit," Sikes said after swallowing.

"We've been looking at this all wrong. It was a farm. Kapelos was their supply chain. Aelfric Tauler was the Master Vampire behind this. He was a farmer, not a hunter."

"Vs are predators. Top of the food chain predators. Like lions," Gram said.

"Tauler hated other vampires that had predator drives. Worst of all, he was *using this team* to find those vampires that wouldn't follow his orders."

Everyone let this sink in.

"Coffee has been on the team for almost three years," Sloan stated. He took another huge bite of meat lover's pizza and chewed, thinking.

"We were at the oil rig," Beck said.

"Where are Franklin and Kapelos?"

Beck exchanged glances with Hodge and Sikes as if deciding something. "Kapelos is dead, and Franklin is at the oil…"

He looked at Sikes again. He shook his head as if to clear it. *If Sikes was here, where is…*

Beck looked, and the whole team was present.

Who's watching Coffee?

Beck rushed to the lab trailer. He burst in, but Valmunin was already gone.

"BEEKER!" Beck yelled, and everyone present seemed to wake from their stupor. Coffee was lying on a gurney.

His arms and legs had been torn off at the shoulders and hips.

Valmunin was gone.

19. OFF THE LEASH

They stood looking at what was left of Coffee. He was unconscious.

"Look, it's not your fault," Sikes said. "You couldn't have stopped him. Val did you a favor. Coffee could have easily killed you all and probably would have if this had gone any other way."

"Where's Valmunin?" Sloan demanded.

"Look, he had a bad night as well. He has people to look after," Sikes said.

Hodge spoke in a puzzling tone. "Valmunin could be standing at your elbow, and you may not notice. He's way past, 'These are not the droids you're looking for.' We'd have no chance."

"I know you don't know me," Sikes said. "I can't explain it. But he is on the humans' side. On our side. Tell them, Hodge. What Switch found."

"This is all happening too fast," Hodge said.

"You think shit's not gonna happen faster when they find out this team is off the leash?" Sikes stated. "Tell them."

Beck spoke before Hodge. "We believe we found another farm. Another nest. Another vampire stronghold. It's in a decommissioned Titan missile silo. North of Bismarck, North Dakota, and south of Minot Air Force base."

"Got any recon?" Sloan asked.

"Negative," Beck replied. "The area is even blurred out on Google Earth."

"Weren't you a priest like five minutes ago?" Beeker said, pulling on surgical gloves and looking at Beck.

"What did he just say?" Sikes was incredulous.

"Well, more like 10 minutes ago," Beck replied.

"Oddjob, how long would it take to preflight the Chinook?" Sloan asked about prepping the huge helicopter as he began to walk out of the lab.

"How safe do you want to feel?" Oddjob asked.

"Bring it here to do it. You can check it out while we load what we need. We are evacuating to the Oil Rig. We will need the secure sat uplink gear at a minimum. Plus, the armory. We will split the team between the two."

"I'm riding with Snow!" Gram called out as everyone scattered.

"Beeker, sew him up. Bring what's left."

***

Beck had the time, quickly showered, and changed into clean clothes. He put on his leather jacket and slung the KRISS so it rested at the small of his back. Grabbing his duffel bag, he looked around one last time and grabbed the katana from the corner after a moment's consideration.

When he opened the door, Hodge and Freya stood there.

They placed their bags in the open cargo compartment of Snow's chopper. They watched Beeker and Shack load body bags onto the Chinook.

The Chinook was super loud as it took off. Snow waited with Hodge, Beck, and Sikes. They'd leave when Brick got back with the new burner phones.

Snow looked directly at Sikes and said, "How do we know Coffee wasn't Valmunin's spy? He silenced him awful quick. And now we are all going where he could more conveniently kill the rest of us."

"He could have killed us all here and saved the hassle," Beck said. "Or just let us blunder on and get ourselves killed. He plays the long game. He doesn't think like us, either. Like a Nostradamus long game."

Brick zoomed up on a motorcycle, parked inside the hangar via the small door, and locked it behind himself.

"What makes you say that?" Snow asked.

Sikes butted in, "It was the dogs. He knew he had to move the dogs."

"Dogs?" Snow asked.

"He somehow knew his base was going to be destroyed. Not one of his people was there. Not even his dogs…"

***

The load inside the Chinook was far from well secured. Sloan knew he should have stayed seated and strapped in. Beeker had just told him that Coffee was conscious.

His gurney was well secured. Sloan placed a headset on Coffee.

"Can you hear me?" Sloan said into his mic. The noise canceling in these headsets was effective.

"Yes, sir," Coffee replied.

"Why?" was all Sloan asked.

"Why, what?" Coffee said.

"I thought we were friends," Sloan said.

"We are. What did I do that was so wrong?" Coffee was angry. "I helped this team hunt down these predators—

201

seventeen of them by my count. I spoon-fed most of them to you. Isn't that what you wanted?"

"You're one of them," Sloan said, stating the obvious.

"I'm NOT like him." Coffee was insulted. "Look at me. That thing isn't like me. He is a monster, a blood heretic! He is the one using you. I was helping you. When he's done with you, what do you think will happen? What do you think he'd do to you if he betrayed his own kind?"

"Aelfric Tauler is dead. The Lodge is in ruins," Sloan said. "It's over."

Coffee's eyes went wide. Sloan took off his headset and went back to his seat.

***

They took off in Snow's Bell 525 and still got there first by a half hour. The sky was clear, and the seas were calm.

Brick had access to the central servers quickly, and the encrypted satellite link was established before midnight.

The crew quarters on the oil rig had four bunks in each and a private bath and shower. It was like a prison facility. The mess hall, rec room, and weight room were all industrial gray.

The former control room for the facility was rapidly converted to the Command Center. It was one of the few things better than their Entenmann's trailer.

It was all simple to bring back online. Even the radar still worked.

"No one can sneak up on us here very easily, at least," Tank said.

"Kinda tough to get pizza delivered," Chan complained.

"Coffee carried a lot of weight on this team," Brick said. "It will take me a long time to get us back up to speed. A fixed base like this will make a lot of things easier. Except for the pizza."

"It's clear Switch thought this Titan base was worth investigating. It's huge," Beck said as he paged through the archived real estate listing.

"It's also 1500 miles away. I think Buffalo is the farthest west we've been for missions. Logistics alone will be…" Sloan was interrupted.

"Logistics?" Hodge nearly shouted. "I thought you saw those girls in the shipping containers. Girls! Can you guess why they pick girls? You're worried about logistics and pizza delivery?"

She slammed a chair out of her way and exited the command center. Sikes stood and followed in the direction Hodge had taken while shaking her head.

Sloan looked Beck in the face and said, "You seem to be the one getting traction around here. What do you recommend?"

"Send your four best recon specialists to Bismarck with local IDs on commercial airlines tomorrow. They rent SUVs and buy guns and gear locally from four different gun stores while wearing Minnesota Viking or Hawaiian shirts from Salvation Army or Goodwill. FBI/SIU Badges are good, but don't use them because the FBI field office there would take umbrage and potentially make your life hard. The field office is in Fargo, by the way. This team has no contacts there, unlike here—no top cover. Have a look. Assess and report."

"You've thought this out already?" Sloan said.

"I had a long talk with Sikes. There were over a hundred perimeter guards at the Lodge. Not just the seven that were still there. The others must have fled. Humans. They were totally unaware of what they were guarding. There were dogs.

There are no motion sensors, though. But the entire perimeter was surrounded by a continuous metal detector. They were waiting for him. For Valmunin.

"We may be looking at the same setup here. Maybe even the same security firm," Beck added. "It's your team. I'm going to bed."

Sloan nodded at Brick, and the wheels began to turn.

***

Hodge was sitting on a lower bunk in her room. Someone had put a piece of blue painter's tape on the door and written HODGE on it with black Sharpie. There was a knock, and the door opened inward without Hodge acknowledging.

"Get out. I need sleep. Why are you even here?" Hodge said, beginning to unlace her boots.

"I'm just here for the hot guys," Sikes said, trying to stay deadpan.

Hodge cracked a smile and shook her head. She went back to taking her boots off.

"You ever been in a fight? I mean a real one. No rules kinda fight," Sikes asked.

Hodge paused for an instant as the smile fell away from her face. "Yes, a few times. I was a cop in fucking Newark, New Jersey."

"You ever lose? In a real fight?" Sikes was severe as well. "Even once."

Hodge fell silent.

"Goodnight, Hodge." Sikes paused before closing the door. "Silk is a stupid nickname. Don't pick that." The door closed behind her.

***

"Wakey, wakey," followed by the lights coming on full, was not how Beck liked to wake up. But with his arm covering his eyes, he could smell coffee.

"What time is it?" Beck sat up and found a mug of strong coffee under his nose.

"0845. That's a quarter to nine in the morning to non-military types," Hodge said as he sipped. "Nice boxers."

"Jesus, you could raise the dead with this stuff." He took another longer sip. "It's horrible. I love it. What's going on?" Beck dry-scrubbed his face with his free hand.

"Tank, Chen, Gram, and Book are on their way to Bismarck," Hodge said before sipping her own coffee and sitting at the desk chair. "Sloan contacted Betty, and she arranged for a cook and janitor. Snow is bringing them back with her. Thank God. I brought you breakfast before Oddjob ate it all. Spam and powdered eggs. You should eat it before it gets cold. Seriously."

Beck got dressed and went up one level to drop off his plate and fork. Oddjob was doing the dishes. He looked far too big to be doing dishes, or even just handling dishes.

"More coffee," Oddjob said and gestured with his head to a massive stainless-steel percolator. Beck poured another cup and ascended the stairs directly into the command center.

"Good morning, sir," Beck said to Sloan, who was standing around a large light table that usually displayed sea charts but now had floor plans of some kind. On closer examination, it was the Titan Missile Installation.

"Morning. Top of your agenda today is this." Sloan pushed a foot-round metal ring across the table to him. The ring itself was about an inch thick.

"What is it?" He picked it up.

"It's a choice. Either Franklin wears this, or she's gone," Sloan said. "It's a new proximity collar. An upgrade from the one that killed Kapelos. This one is also a shock collar. It will incapacitate before killing. If she leaves the lab, it will explode. If she pisses me off, I have a remote trigger. If it isn't on her neck in 30 minutes, she goes over the side, gurney and all."

Beck understood the reasons.

"Any reason you didn't send me and Hodge to Bismarck?" he asked.

"You aren't a recon specialist. They are. And that's how we normally work around here. Collect intel, then act. You ever hear of an OODA loop? Observe–Orient–Decide–Act."

"No, but that's kinda what I've been doing since I got here," Beck said. "I should add sleep in that loop. A SOODA loop. Makes the rest of it easier."

He took the collar and moved into the hallway. It hinged open and closed easily, and there was only a single flush button marked ACTIVATE. It was way bigger than a human neck. It would even fit on Oddjob. Maybe.

Hodge was in the lab talking to Franklin when he opened the door. Franklin was once again in full restraints.

"Last night, Sloan almost retired Franklin," Hodge said. "He was persuaded to let you decide."

Franklin said nothing. She would not even look at him. He stepped up to her, and with a physical key, he removed the old collar.

"I presume you know this is what killed Kapelos." He set it aside. "Here is the deal. No one trusts you. You must understand that. So, if you want to live, you'll have to earn our trust again. Until then you'll have to wear this. Do you know what this is?"

Franklin looked over finally. She saw the new collar and nodded yes, causing fresh tears to spill.

Beck approached her and held it up, opened. She raised her head from the gurney. He closed it around her neck and pressed activate. It slowly slid into itself. The activate button disappeared into the collar as it slid into itself. The resizing stopped before it was too tight. Fingers could slide beneath it.

"You'll be restricted to the lab. You'll have to follow orders," Beck said.

"I know how slavery works," Franklin sobbed.

"Don't say that again!" Beck barked. "Coffee almost killed us all yesterday. Coffee, Rodney Jones, was a Stage Two vampire the whole time! Spying on the team. Manipulating us. How are we supposed to know if you weren't with him? Part of that!"

Franklin's eyes were wide. She didn't know or she was the best actress ever.

Beck turned to storm out. Before he got to the door, Franklin said, "Beck. It's not activated all the way until you set the perimeter and arm it from the remote."

He paused but didn't look back. Hodge followed him out.

***

Their plane arrived at 9:05 am, and their rented Tahoe and Escalade were both dark blue. They visited Salvation Army next and obtained t-shirts, and to their surprise, Gram looked amazing in yoga pants, a Mötley Crüe t-shirt, and sneakers.

The next stop was gun stores. They picked four different gun shops, and whoever was buying went alone in their vehicle while the other three waited elsewhere. Savvy gun shop owners watched for people waiting outside in the car. It sometimes indicated straw purchasers that were prohibited persons. The state had no waiting periods for purchases.

They were rolling and geared up by noon.

They parked the vehicles in a clearing off the road and out of sight about a kilometer away from the installation. They left their phones in the SUVs inside Faraday bags. They'd be doing this recon quietly. Their radios were set on receive only and would only transmit in an emergency. Gram also had a multi-frequency scanner that could passively receive and record anything else.

They knew the plan. They'd rendezvous back at the SUVs in 24 hours. The camo they wore over their new clothes was the only clothes they brought with them.

They melted into the woods.

It was easy to locate the edge of the compound using an advanced GPS. A rusty fence lined the edge. Following a deer trail, Gram traversed along the old fence, finding several places where the fence was open or even collapsed.

Inside, the fence was completely overgrown. They were lucky there was no snow on the ground, and it wasn't too cold. The grasses were taller than her head. Scrub trees were growing where they should be mowed tight for visibility.

Eventually, per the plan, she found the main gate. It was overgrown with vines and hadn't been closed in decades. The blacktop was faded and cracked, with weeds growing up out of it.

Roofs of buildings could be seen about 300 yards away. Movement caught Gram's eye. Through binoculars, she saw an old man in dirty denim coveralls. He had a long, dirty gray beard and wispy hair. He walked into a rusty Quonset hut, and a few minutes later, she heard an engine start. He was now wearing a wide-brimmed straw hat and riding a John Deere lawn mower down the road toward Gram's position.

She'd been standing in the tall grass on a well-worn deer trail. She left the path and lay down where she could see the road just beyond the vines of the fence.

The mower was smaller than the amount of noise it made. A large black plastic bag was balanced on the hood of the green tractor. Oblivious to her presence, he drove straight by, not glancing side to side while keeping one hand on the bag. The sound of the motor faded into the distance for another couple of minutes and stopped.

Gram stood and crouched as she carefully moved to the grass at the very edge of the road. Through her binocs, she watched him at a distant mailbox. Beside the mailbox was a trash can with its lid hinged open. The black plastic bag was gone from the hood of the mower, and he was opening several pieces of mail and after a short glance at each letter, tossed them into the trash can.

Last, he pulled a newspaper from a yellow tube below the mailbox and tucked it under his arm. Adjusting his hat, he climbed back onto his lawn tractor and headed back.

Gram didn't retreat into the weeds as far this time. He passed by her position again less than ten yards from her. He drove the mower directly into the Quonset hut.

Exiting the open overhead door, he walked back across the open parking area to an attached porch on another structure. He set the newspaper on top of a window air conditioning unit and went inside.

Gram retrieved her camera and long lens from her small backpack. With the tripod set, the extreme magnification was steady. She watched him come out with a can of beer. He retrieved the newspaper and set both down on a cable spool repurposed as an end table. He sat on a folding lawn chair and lit a cigar.

She watched him sit, smoke, read the paper, and sip his beers for hours. At one point, he got up and peed off the far end of the porch before retrieving another beverage.

At dusk, he dumped his cans and emptied his ashtray into a large galvanized bucket with a lid that had seen better days.

Gram got a few good photos of him. Front and profile. She photographed the building as well. She settled in for a long night.

A single street light came on with the darkness. Lights were on inside the house for a while. The glow of a TV filled the front room until 0200.

It was incredibly quiet. At 0230, Gram decided to have a walk about when the wind picked up. One of the only pieces of gear she brought on the trip was her high-end night vision goggles. She put them on and activated them.

She was shocked by what she saw.

There were hundreds of infrared light sources. Floodlights and cameras became apparent, including one above and behind her.

FUCK.

She clicked the mic three times rapidly, three times in a row. It was the signal that the operation was blown and to retreat with all possible speed.

She was silently packed and moving in 30 seconds. Her night vision served her well. She was able to run full tilt. She could hear someone behind her crashing through the woods with less finesse.

There was gunfire in the distance. It was loud in the hush of the night.

Then she heard suppressed gunfire behind her. Bullets were whizzing by her as adrenaline poured into her veins. A round grazed her right ear.

Suppressors are never as quiet as you think.

A round impacted the armor plate that protected her back. She saw her chance. She executed a well-practiced roll that looked like she'd stumbled and fallen when she'd landed in a perfect prone position, presenting a minimal target. When she saw him on his continued rush ahead, she opened fire. The AR15 was loud in the night. The muzzle flashes were bright. He went down and was dead before he hit the ground right in front of Gram.

Without hesitation, she stripped him of his suppressed HK MP5 and an extra magazine. She was running again. Two kilometers had never seemed so far. She'd been running full out for ten minutes, which felt like an hour. She crouched in heavy undergrowth and practiced disciplined breathing. She knew exhaling was essential to clear the CO2 as quickly as possible.

She noticed her radio was vibrating against her skin. She drew it out and looked at it in horror.

The display read Alpha 4, Alpha 2, and Alpha 3. Tank, Book, and Chen were all dead. She felt for the recon patch under her left arm that monitored her heart for one reason. To let the rest of the team know that it had stopped beating and to scramble the radio so captors couldn't use it. She tore the patch off.

She heard the dirt bike on the path long before she saw it. The headlight was not infrared, and the fool wasn't wearing a helmet. She swung the AR15 like a baseball bat catching him full in the face. The motorcycle crashed into the trees and stalled. The headlight shattered.

Quiet fell again on the darkness. She searched his body. She collected everything without examining anything. She even took his wallet.

Dumbass amateur carrying a wallet?

She had the motorcycle up and started rapidly. When she cleared the woods and found a road, she fled. Several turns led her to some railroad tracks that she followed until they intersected an interstate. Only then did she pause and check her location. It was 3 am.

She opted to follow the train tracks to Fargo. The bus station was not far from the tracks. She hid the dirt bike behind a freshly emptied dumpster. She stowed the MP5 and her Glock in her backpack with her goggles. The rest went into the dumpster. She stripped down to her yoga pants, t-shirt, and coat and combed the French braid out of her hair. She purchased a bus ticket to Cleveland, Ohio that left in 22 minutes, using cash. She bought a large coffee, two sausage egg and cheese sandwiches, and a *People* magazine.

Calmly, she absorbed her surroundings, pretended to read her magazine, ate her sandwiches, and boarded the bus as the last one on.

She didn't go to Cleveland. She left the bus in Madison, Wisconsin. At 3 p.m., she called Sloan on the secure line. It was the prearranged time to check-in.

She gave a quick report.

By the time her cab arrived at the Dane County Regional Airport, a private jet had been chartered to bring her directly to Newark, where Snow and Sloan were waiting with the Chopper.

Gram stood before Sloan and said, "I'm sorry, Chief."

Sloan simply gathered her into a hug. She remained stiff.

***

The oil rig base had been renamed Utah Base. Sloan was not able to figure out the moment it happened. He also had no idea how the conference table fit onto the Chinook with all the other gear.

A stripped machine shop had been converted to the team's conference room on Utah Base.

It had been three days since Gram had returned, and she was still angry. The bodies of Tank, Chan, and Book hadn't surfaced yet.

"We had some hard lessons. Dealing with Farmers is very different than Hunters. Farmers use humans for tech and security. Without realizing it, Gram got photos of the surveillance cameras at the silo." Sloan dimmed the lights and brought up an image on the screen. It was a composite of several cameras. All were carefully painted to hide them in their surroundings. "All of these are from Brime Tech and super high-end. We won't make that mistake again."

Beck stood and continued the briefing, "We've had a breakthrough regarding the silo. This was due to the cross-referencing of three things Gram collected on-site. First is the MP5 she collected. It's a Class 3, full-auto, 9mm, with a high-end suppressor. They're very highly controlled and cost about $30,000 each. Two, the wallet and driver's license of Kyle McDonald, his actual name. And three, these two photos of this man."

The high-def photos Gram took of his front and profile were displayed above. Albert Shockley was displayed on military ID photos.

"Turns out Kyle McDonald had gotten married and not told anyone. His parents were notified of his accidental death in a motorcycle crash. When I called and told his wife I was a friend from work, Kyle had confided in me about her. She straight up asked if vampires did this. She'd begged him to quit the team. She even named Shockley as the team lead."

Sloan broke in, "I think we walked into another team like us. Waiting to collect more vampires."

20. SHOCKLEY

Shockley walked to the specified parking garage level and row. The message he'd received included a key and fob—standard team protocol. The car was easy to find with the press of a button. Instructions would be in the glove box, as always. When he got to the driver's door, it was still locked. He tried the fob again as the taser needles entered his back. Before his knees could buckle, the side door of the van parked behind him slid open, and strong arms collected him.

Before reason returned, he'd been disarmed, stripped of all his comms, and cuffed and zip-tied to a wheelchair in the back of the van with a black bag over his head.

"He's awake, chief," Oddjob said.

"ETA four minutes." Gram said, anger dripping from her voice.

"We'll just let him wake up a bit more. Test his bonds. Let him be certain about his situation," Sloan said.

For the next four minutes, he made no secret of testing how securely he was fucked.

The van was out in the plains, east of the airport. It pulled into an abandoned farm and parked behind the barn hidden from the road.

Sloan had them carry out the wheelchair and place it so the van was at his back, hiding the rented chopper beyond.

Gram yanked off his hood a bit over-zealously.

"Albert Shockley, the legendary leader of the Denver vampire hunters. I read all about what happened in Santa Fe. Messy. Difficult to cover up. Sloppy, really." Sloan held out his hand, and Hodge put a file folder into it.

"Fifty-one years old, divorced from Mary Shockley, who now lives on Paris Street in Denver, no children. Two younger sisters, one lives in Boulder with two kids still in high school, two older daughters married, and two small children. And your other sister Kate that…"

"OK, I get it. I talk, or you'll kill my whole family," Shockley said. Looking at Gram, he continued, "She killed two of my men! They had families!"

"You killed *three* of my men," Gram growled. "They. Were. Family."

Sloan smiled. "You misunderstand me, Albert. May I call you Albert?" He closed the file and handed it to Hodge. She exchanged it for a K-Bar knife. "I'm not going to kill you and your family. I think I may just be able to save them. You see, I'm the leader of the Hunter team much like yours, but stationed in Newark. And we've just discovered vampires are controlling our missions. Mine AND yours."

With that, he began cutting the zip ties that bound him.

***

It took just over two hours to run it all down for Shockley. The Farmers knew Switch had discovered the silo. It had been evacuated. After that, Shockley's team had been staking out the silo for two months, told that vampires would be returning in force. The Denver team also had a comms officer addicted to a hot beverage—Red Rose tea in this case.

"Her name is Marcy Abrams. She's an Indian."

"From India?" Oddjob asked.

"No. American Indian. Seneca, I think. You know. A squaw. She is our lead comm officer and tech. A workaholic," Shockley said. This caused a lull in the conversation.

"Where are the bodies of my men?" Gram had been patient and waited for the discussion to have a random pause. It was the sound of wrath, barely contained.

"They're back at our lab. It's a mobile lab in a hangar at Denver Airport. We thought they were Stage One vampires. I'm sorry. We didn't know." Shockley was sincere.

The apology caused an instant change in Gram. "I, too, am sorry. We thought you were human traffickers. Murderers. Vampires." She bowed her head to him for a moment. A single tear slipped down her cheek and off her chin when she looked up. She didn't wipe it away.

***

"Have you ever seen one of these?" Sloan handed Shockley the thermal scanner.

"No. But we use a variant for security. Ours are fixed-point cameras. No automation, though. They need a person watching."

"And who is assigned this task?" Sloan asked.

"Shit. Abrams," Shockley said. "You're telling me that someone I've worked with, literally for years, is probably a Stage Two vampire?"

"Maybe a Stage Three," Sloan said. "To her, being hundreds of years old, a three-year job will feel like a week to us. Does she disappear once a week for a few hours?"

"She has to do her own laundry herself, at a specific laundromat every time. Special soap or some OCD shit," Shockley said, pulling on his beard as he talked.

"That's when she is given fresh blood. She'll gorge herself on just over two gallons of human blood," Sloan stated as fact. Does she use a lot of lotion on her skin? Unscented? You know how their skin degrades over time. They know how to protect their skin now."

"Look… If you're right about this…" Shockley was thinking hard. "I'd rather be stuck in that command trailer with a pissed-off grizzly bear that's on cocaine. How can you be sure without giving it away?"

"Leave that to us." Sloan then gestured to his left. "I'd like you to meet Officer Maris Hodge. And her bomb-sniffing dog, Freya."

She wore a black polo shirt and plain khaki slacks with a windbreaker that said DENVER PD K-9 UNIT on the back. Her badge was hanging on a lanyard around her neck.

The dog was huge but had a goofy expression as it panted with her tongue hanging out the side. Hodge introduced the dog. "This is Freya. As far as I know, the only vampire-sniffing dog that exists. She can let us be sure."

"Abrams loves dogs," Shockley said.

"All the better," Sloan said. "So, here's the plan…"

They laid it out to Shockley in detail. It was a simple plan. It relied heavily on Shockley's crew following orders, or Hodge was at risk.

"What if there's more than one vampire on the crew?" Shockley asked. "Didn't you say the doc was also a vampire?"

"She did that to herself," Sloan said.

"And you believe she's not with them?" Shockley asked.

"Yes," Sloan and Hodge said at once.

"OK, but let's be careful. I'm questioning everything now," Shockley said as he got behind the wheel of the van. Officer Maris Hodge and Freya were passengers.

***

The van pulled up in front of a private hangar with big doors closed. They parked next to a black Suburban, a yellow taxi, and a Ford F-150 pickup. The only thing they had in common was the tinted glass.

Shockley led them in through the side door, and Hodge had major *déjà vu*. The hanger had a helicopter parked in the center. There were half a dozen RVs, an Airstream, and three unmarked tractor-trailers. Hodge wondered where the conference table was.

They walked up the eerily similar steps to enter a command trailer that seemed to have rolled off the same assembly line as theirs.

There were two people inside the command trailer at different stations. "This is Abrams and Alcott. Meet Officer Maris Hodge of the Denver PD K-9 unit," said Shockley. "And this is Freya, her bomb-sniffing dog. Marcy, can you call everyone together, all shifts? I'd like to only go over this once. Alcott, can you go out and fire up the big screen? Marcy can monitor from in here."

Freya was lying on the floor as if she was about to fall asleep.

"All crew, please assemble in the lounge for a quick meeting in five minutes," Abrams announced. Several acknowledgements came in rapidly.

"Up, girl," Hodge said as Freya stood, looking at Abrams wearing her goofy face.

"Can I pet her?" Abrams spun her chair around and held a hand out to the dog.

"Sure, Freya, it's OK. Off duty."

Freya rushed up, sniffed Abrams, then gave her a lick, and got an ear scratch in return.

"Marcy, do you know what this is?" Shockley asked as he held up a red aluminum device the size of a pack of cigarettes with two six-inch long antennas.

"Well?" Hodge said to Freya.

Marcy barely glanced up from the dog. "Yes, That's an all-band signal jammer. Make sure you don't activate that in here…"

Shockley switched it on.

Abrams didn't notice Hodge's Smith & Wesson .500 magnum, even though the long vented barrel on the gun made it huge. The first shot blew her right arm off at the shoulder.

Abrams looked at the dog. Its teeth were bared, and its right paw pointed at her chest.

It took two shots to remove the other arm and one to remove her right leg below the knee. Each shot slammed her into the console behind her. The arms of the chair kept her from falling out.

She didn't bleed. A thick honey-like substance oozed out. Her face was in shock.

Shockley heard feet on the metal steps and intercepted them at the door before they could enter.

"It's all right. As you were," Shockley ordered, and two men holstered their Glocks and turned around as Freya rushed past them. Hodge threw Abrams, chair and all, off the back of the stairs to crash below.

The entire crew knew what an advanced-stage vampire looked like.

"As of right now, we are in a full comms blackout and base lockdown," Shockley shouted over the crew's heads.

Freya crashed into a thin lab coat-wearing man from behind. He stumbled onto his face with the dog's full weight on him. He rolled back to his feet with enough speed and force to send Freya flying.

Shockley began firing as people dived away, hitting the man six times in the chest before he launched himself from the floor to land on the roof of the lab trailer.

Hodge fired, blowing a leg clean off at the knee and sending him over the far side.

"What have you got in there?" Shockley asked Hodge as they ran to the other side of the trailer.

"It's a hot load of .500 magnum, explosive point depleted uranium," Hodge said as they rounded the corner to find nothing. Returning, they found Abrams had rolled onto her back, revealing the extent of her wounds. Her left arm was gone, and her collarbone. It revealed a portion of her open chest cavity and ruined lung.

"Who are you?" she whispered. The light was already fading from her eyes.

"Not who. What." Hodge knelt low so only Shockley and Abrams could hear. "You'll tell me what I want to know, or I will encase you in cement and throw you into the deepest ocean where lies only hunger and insanity."

She only lived another fifteen minutes, but it was enough time. Shockley ordered the base searched, and comm bugs and location devices were found.

His entire team was boarding their now bug-free chopper as Snow, Sloan, Beck, and Gram were landing to pick up Hodge, Freya, and three body bags.

***

The two choppers flew to the abandoned farm out in the plains. The remains of both teams were there. Shockley explained to the Denver crew the situation with Sloan's help. They asked important questions. The proof was there at their feet in the open-body bag. Beck thought they took it quite well, considering. Shockley's remaining crew was eight men and two women. All stoic. Angry but well-disciplined.

"Abrams hated her handlers more than she hated us," Shockley said. "She tried to fuck them over in the end. She said there were six teams like us in North America. All are being manipulated like us. By vampires."

"What if she was lying?" A woman on the crew asked.

"It's a possibility. But she told us one other thing. The most important thing. Where the mastermind is located." Before Shockley could finish, the crew pointed out into the plain.

A chopper was moving toward them at high speed. It was close to the ground and leaning into it. It prop-washed and slowed at the last possible moment, setting down like a rescue chopper in a hurry. The tail was pointed at the crew, obscuring who the pilot was. A side door slid open, and a man in a white coat was thrown out onto the grass, face down.

The man had only one leg.

A tall blond woman jumped out and stood over the man with the point of a katana held to the base of his neck.

Everyone was frozen when the pilot rounded the nose of the chopper. He seemed to walk to the man on the ground in slow motion. Reaching down, he lifted the man up by his neck. Not the scruff of his shirt—his hand circumnavigated his entire throat. The man struggled, but his arms were bound behind his back. He looked like a child by comparison.

Many of Shockley's team drew side arms when they noticed the doc wasn't bleeding.

Valmunin threw him to the ground in their midst. "Tell them," came the command. The doctor began to speak rapidly.

"I had leukemia. It's why I became a blood disease specialist. I was already on the crew by the time it started getting worse. When I thought I only had a few months left, I did a Hail Mary. I had access to blood without costing lives. Check my laptop. I logged it all in a diary. I'm not one of them. I'm with you. Please don't kill me. I've gone through so much to live…" He was sobbing.

"Sound familiar?" Beck said to Sloan.

"Mother fucking lying bitch… I defended her," Hodge said.

"Who the hell are you talking about? I want to know about him." Shockley pointed at Valmunin with a shaking hand.

Valmunin's eyes were glowing as he studied every member of both groups. His t-shirt was sleeveless, and his skin was so thin his muscle strands looked like steel cables under stress, barely beneath the surface.

"Oh, him? That's Beck's assistant. Please don't shoot him. It might piss him off," Sloan said deadpan.

As the guns lowered and were holstered, Valmunin seemed to cool. His eyes dimmed. He didn't seem so tall. He walked over, slid a boot under the doc's shoulder, and rolled him onto his side.

Beck noticed then that his arms weren't merely tied behind his back. In several places, a thick steel cable had been stabbed through his forearms between ulna and radius bones on each arm.

"We know about you—the truth," said Sloan. "Abrams told us everything. Not your bullshit story. I just wanted to give you one last chance to fuck over the ones that betrayed you."

"I was sick. There was nothing else I could do…"

Valmunin held out his hand. Sikes placed the katana's handle into his palm but held the scabbard as he drew the sword.

"Wait. I know where they are. All the farms in North America. ALL our orders come from that one place."

"Abrams also told us. She also said she wasn't supposed to know. If you speak the truth, you may still survive this day. Unlike Abrams."

"Pleasant Valley. Near Fresno. Well, it's not near anything. It's a prison in the middle of the fucking desert. Nothing near it. No getting out, no getting in. There's a secret facility below the East Annex, the Palace they call it." He was speaking fast. "There's secret tunnel access from the orchard. I can help you."

The doc was gushing. "The prison is the biggest farm I've ever seen. The Warden is a vampire, too. Some guards, too. I used to work in the hospital there. Two thousand seven hundred prisoners plus the girls in the Palace below."

"Do with him what you will." Valmunin turned and began to walk away. Sikes was there and tried to stop him with the scabbard held in both hands across his chest. It looked like she was trying to stop a moving train. Her feet were sliding back across the grass.

"Wait. Let them help. Let us help. We can help." Sikes was adamant. Beck couldn't believe she had the courage to do that.

"I've been there before. I know the Orchard Tunnel. In '95, it was no palace. We need to act. Before they run, they always run," Valmunin said.

"Think of the Lodge, all the planning. That almost went sideways." Sikes talked to him like he was a human—a man.

"I know you're tired. I know." Sikes backed away, and he stood like a statue. "I know you don't know them. Let them help."

"There's more," Doc said from the ground. "She's an ancient hag they call the Vrabia—the Black Sparrow. There are a ton more scary names. All I know is that no one I know has ever seen her and lived. The ancient hag ordered that all of you be killed and you be burned. She was using you, just like she was using the teams. For centuries. All of us."

"The Keep is all I've left that she has never touched," he growled.

"You promised I could see it," Sikes said just as Freya approached and pushed her face into Valmunin's hand.

Valmunin sighed and the spell broke. Valmunin released them. Everyone could breathe again.

"Who is this hag, Vrabia?" Sloan asked.

"I don't know, but I soon will," Valmunin said, and after a pause, he turned to his chopper. "Gentlemen, you'll need to follow me closely, or you'll be shot down."

"Saddle up, people!" Both Sloan and Shockley said at the same time. The teams mixed and began introducing themselves without being asked as they piled into the choppers.

No one mentioned Valmunin collecting Abrams's body bag. Beck knew why. He'd feed.

"You have a Stage Three on your team. I gotta get me one of those," someone said.

"Can ours be a woman?" The machismo of the tactical team was back.

Beck thought they were rolling with it better than he believed they would and said so to Hodge.

"I've never seen people more able to roll with shit," Hodge replied. "Except maybe if he was a priest ten minutes ago."

***

The flight was harrowing.

In the Rockies, they flew into a maze of canyons.

"I'd wish he'd slow the fuck down. This isn't Begger's Canyon back home," Snow said through gritted teeth. Even though she thought she was following too close, she'd lose sight of Valmunin's chopper around the cliffs.

Charts did her no good as they couldn't keep up. She had to turn off the ground proximity alarm because it constantly screamed.

"Of all the Captain Crunch shit, we've now entered restricted air space," Snow said.

"Cheyenne Mountain? You gotta be shitting me!" Hodge said.

"Where the fuck are we going?" They turned into a blind canyon and almost crashed into Valmunin's chopper. Snow flew over it, and Shockley flew under it. In the cliff wall before them was a tower that looked like it was part of the mountain. A wide natural shelf flanked the tower to each side with a sheer wall drop of hundreds of feet below where a small river flowed.

A camouflaged Vietnam-era Huey was already parked on the shelf. Valmunin gestured for first one, then the other, to land. When both had landed, Valmunin landed on the roof of the tower, trimming a few leaves as he did.

Hodge stepped out and looked up. She could see no sky. The choppers were hidden even from a passing plane between the rock overhang and the opposite cliff face.

They exited the helicopters as if on a mission—slung rifles held in low ready. The entire crew formed up and awaited orders.

A lone figure walked out of a stone arch that was in a ten-foot-tall stone wall. Flagstones could be seen beyond.

"Greetings, I'm Takashi. You're safe here. Please follow me." He bowed, turned on his heel, and entered the arch.

The courtyard beyond was a beautiful garden. Flagstones made a path through small moss-covered hills with dwarf trees of several varieties. Water that flowed down the cliff was collected in a pond by the wall. A beautifully designed brook flowed through the garden, making a restful babbling. Benches were beside the paths, and they crossed a small bridge over the brook as the path flowed toward the front door.

They entered and were surprised it was warm inside. Antique gaslight provided illumination in the vast, single room. The ceiling was probably fifteen feet high, but Hodge thought it felt low because of the size of the room.

The next surprise was that every wall was covered with bookcases, all full and tidy enough to make any librarian proud.

An avalanche of dogs flowed down the stairs with Freya in the lead. All had tails wagging and greeted everyone in search of ear scratches that were freely given, even though they were mostly intimidating Dobermans and Rottweilers.

Sikes descended the stairs with an older, strikingly beautiful Asian woman.

"Aiko, this is Trevor Sloan and Albert Shockley," Sikes said. "I'll call them the Crew Chiefs. They'll have to introduce the rest. Val will be down in a few minutes."

In accented but perfect English, Aiko said, "We weren't expecting you, so dinner will be simple fare and ready in an hour." She then issued a command to the dogs, "Jiā," sending them all back up the stairs except Freya, who sat perfectly next to Hodge.

"Thank you for your hospitality, Aiko," Shockley said in a ham-handed flirt.

"Thank you, Aiko. Can we assist?" Sloan said.

She smiled and said, "I will call when it's ready. Dining is one level up." She turned and ascended the stairs, oblivious to her traditional silk Qupao Mandarin gown's effect on men such as these.

"Yikes," Hodge said under her breath.

"Tell me about it." Sikes was shaking her head. "Make yourself at home, folks."

"Sheesh, I never expected Vs to like to read," Snow said. "If I were doomed to be immortal, I'd finally have enough time to read."

"Doomed?" Sikes asked.

Beck replied without thinking. "It's a curse. Micah 7:2 – The good men perish out of the earth: and there's no good or upright among these men. They all lie in wait for blood; they hunt every man and his brother as if with a net."

"That's from the Bible?" Sikes asked.

"Yes," Beck replied. "And there's Proverbs 30:14 — *There's a generation whose teeth are like swords, And whose fangs are like knives, To devour the poor from off the earth, And the needy from among men.*"

"Jesus Christ," Sikes said. "It really says that?"

"Yes, and much more," Beck continued. "Leviticus 17:10-14 — And whatsoever man there be of the house of Israel, or of the strangers that sojourn among them, that eat any manner of blood, I will set my face against that soul that consume blood, and will cut him off from among his people."

"Beck was a priest five minutes ago," Hodge quipped.

"A lifetime ago," Beck replied with a hint of sadness.

Beck turned, and Gram was standing there. "Sir, what about… the bodies?"

Sikes overheard the question. "Master Takashi," followed by rapid Japanese.

"Hai," was his reply, and he bowed to Gram.

"Takashi will assist you. He'll meet you at the chopper with help," Sikes said as kindly as she could. Gram followed him out.

Two other men came in at the same time. To Shockley, they said, "Sir, um… he took the Doc. He… umm… ignored us. Almost like an afterthought, he said. He said he had a cell in the Keep, and we could join the others."

"Go on. Make yourself at home," Shockley said, shaking his head. To Sloan, he said, "What the hell are we doing?"

"If I had to guess, we are breaking into a prison tomorrow," Sloan replied.

21. PLEASANT VALLEY

"I hate this plan," Sloan said. "Too many unknowns. Too many bluffs."

"It's all we got. But why our real names?" Gram said as she rolled down the window.

"We are bait. If he knows who we are, he is more likely to believe the rest," Sloan answered.

"They actually named this prison 'Pleasant Valley'?" Gram asked but got no answer as they rolled up to the gate.

"IDs, please," the guard said.

"Trevor Sloan and Diana Aubrey here to see Warden Chandler." Gram handed the guard their SIU IDs with their real names.

The guard scanned them as he called in. Gram put the car into park, trying not to look at the overcast night sky.

"The guard returned the IDs and said, "Follow the signs to Admin parking. Spot #3, and leave this on your dash while on the compound. The Warden's assistant will meet you and show you the way up. Have a good evening." The iron gate began to slide aside slowly.

Standing in front of parking space number three was a young man in a cheap suit with glasses and a tablet hugged to his chest.

They exited the car and were greeted with a limp handshake and a 'right this way' from "David."

Inside the lobby, there were two more guards behind a thick glass wall.

"Any weapons, knives, metal objects go into the lockers there. Take the key with you. Please don't lose it," the bored guard recited.

Gram and Sloan unholstered their Stainless Desert Eagles. They removed the magazine and cleared the round in the chamber, leaving the slides locked back. They slid the guns into the locker.

Sloan added two additional magazines and a pocket knife. Gram added three magazines, a six-inch fixed-blade knife from the small of her back, and then a compact Glock 26 from an ankle holster.

"You guys travel light," the guard kidded. Gram didn't crack a smile. She locked the locker, placed her iPhone, keys, and wristwatch all into a Tupperware bowl, and walked through the metal detector arch. She collected her things as Sloan did the same.

David led them up to the fourth floor and the Warden's corner office. They were introduced, and David left them, closing the door.

"Please sit." Warden Chandler gestured to the chairs in front of the desk.

"I'm sorry, sir, but our business can't wait for pleasantries," Sloan said, drawing out his phone and bringing up a photo. He slid it across the desk.

My unit was nearly destroyed on a mission yesterday by a… man named Rhys Valmunin. Our team's doctor was severely injured in an escape attempt and recommended we bring him here and speak directly to you in person. In private."

Warden Chandler was looking at the image of forearms cabled together. "You have him here?"

"He is in an unmarked van, not far from here." Sloan sounded genuinely worried. "Word was he was wanted alive, but honestly, I don't know how long we can hold him. We have four Tasers in him now. The batteries are almost dead, and he is waking. He has been shot so many times we've lost count. It wasn't until we took his eyes that we gained the advantage. Now, even they're healing. Like the rest. We have to hurry."

Sloan slid to the next photo of a white Ford Transit van. The next was a close-up of the license plate.

"The driver's name is Jim Whitecloud, and he has his SIU credentials with him."

Chandler was immediately on the phone with the gate guards.

"Dan, there's another unscheduled prisoner transfer arriving soon. Please direct them back to the small loading dock." He paused, "Yes, Dock B1. I will personally be meeting them there." He gave the make and model of the van, its plate number, and the driver's name.

Sloan made a call. "We are a go. They're expecting you." Sloan hung up. "Look, Warden. I'm going out on a limb here. I don't know you. But… This guy is a monster. A Stage Four, maybe Five V. Do you know what that is? Are you prepared for this?"

"Mr. Sloan, we are well aware of who and what this individual is. Our super-max has provisions made just for cases like this. Well done in the capture. I look forward to hearing the whole story later."

They were now walking back the way they came. The Warden, now in a hurry as well, spoke into a hand-held radio. "Bring Jackson and a Gray Gurney to Dock B1, on the double." Then to Sloan, "It will be faster if we take your car to B1. Collect your personals, and we'll meet them at the gate."

At the lockers, they collected, reloaded their guns, and collected their items. As they got in the car, Chandler's radio spoke. "We are now at Dock B1, standing by."

When they arrived at the gate, the Warden got out and spoke to the booth guards just as the van pulled up. Gram took a deep breath in through her nose and out her mouth. She looked at her watch.

The gate slid aside, and the van pulled in. The Warden climbed in the back seat of Sloan's car and directed them where to go.

"Sign this before we forget." Gram handed back a clipboard. Protocol required it. The name was listed as John Doe. He signed it with the Sharpie provided and handed it back.

Dock B1, as expected, was secluded, had no cameras, and was surrounded by four-story windowless brick walls on all sides. They even had to drive through a narrow tunnel to get there.

Sloan pulled the car to the side and got out. Two men waited by a heavy steel table with an inch-thick rebar cage. It was open and awaiting its guest.

"Hang on," Sloan said and drew his weapon. "I'm serious about this guy. Don't trust him."

Gram also drew her Desert Eagle and held it ready, pointing at the van door.

The Warden got a thumbs up from Oddjob as the driver's door opened. The men began pushing the gurney closer. The van door began to slide, and just when it was fully open, three shots rang out simultaneously.

Gram shot Warden Chandler point blank in the back of his head at the base of his skull. At the same time, the explosive depleted uranium rounds struck the other two men in the center of their faces. None of the bullets exited their skulls.

The Warden fell face-first into the van. Sloan quickly swung his legs in.

Takashi and Oddjob struggled to carry the first man and then the other to the van.

"I'd guess by the weight alone they were both Stage Twos, at least," Oddjob said, tossing a black blanket over the bodies.

"Shit's going to hit the fan as soon as we're clear. Don't kill any guards if you don't need to." Sloan and Gram got back into their car and led the way out.

Sloan paused at the guard shack and rolled down the window, handing back the parking permit. "Need this back? Jim said he didn't get one, and the prisoner has been transferred." He handed the guard the clipboard. With a yawn, the guard waved both vehicles through.

Sloan picked up a radio from the seat and said the code words that indicated they were clear. "Going to McDonald's. You guys need anything?" There was no reply, but they knew three jumpers exited a plane at 20,000 feet.

"You ever do a HALO jump on a cloudy night?" Sloan casually asked Gram.

"Yes. I didn't mind the extreme altitude, the long fall, the low opening, the night jumps, or the clouds. It was the bone-freezing cold on the way down that always got to me."

Sloan watched the rearview as much as the road. There was no pursuit.

"Things are straight up easier when we just murder these mother fuckers," Gram said.

Sloan knew from the way she said it she wasn't sure.

"They've been killing people for decades, maybe centuries," Sloan said.

"But when I pulled that trigger… I wasn't 100% sure he was… I don't know who to believe anymore, chief. So, I'll just believe you."

She looked at her watch, saying, "Brick is up at bat." Just as the lights went out at the prison, thirty seconds later, as the giant diesel generators kicked on, a series of rockets exploded on the west wall.

***

There was a lucky break in the clouds below. Hodge saw all six rockets impact the wall and the main generator explode. The wall didn't collapse, but it was loud, big, and caused an enormous cloud of dust, and it was all on the far side of the prison.

The drop from 20,000 feet only took a couple of minutes. Their chutes were black and opened at about 800 feet. It only gave them a few seconds to glide to the edge of the east orchard.

The M134 miniguns in the doors of the Huey made quick work of all the spotlights mounted on the towers. The tower guards hit the deck, and then the windows all shattered even though they were "bullet resistant." Hodge didn't know the pilot or the door gunners, but she knew they were at the greatest risk in this whole plan. While trying not to kill any guards, they knew there were guards down there with rifles.

Dozens of tear gas and smoke grenades would be littered over the various yards. They wanted maximum chaos and confusion in one fast pass over the prison. None of the hardware they used was modern. Black market shit that would lead to investigative dead ends. They'd create havoc for three minutes and be gone before police helicopters could be dispatched from Fresno.

The prison alarms were all screaming.

Valmunin came out of the dark while stuffing the last of his chute into a nylon duffle. When Hodge and Sikes were also done, they donned their night vision goggles. They carried black SCAR, suppressed, short-barrel rifles. The advanced ammo filled their vests.

Valmunin carried no weapons, but he did carry a custom Halligan Bar. It was a fireman's combination tool. Part pry bar, part pick axe, part hammer, and all lethal in his hands.

They entered a tractor shed in the northwest corner of the orchard. Valmunin flipped a pallet over with one hand that had two bales of straw. Using the Halligan, the hatch was opened instantly, and he dropped his duffle in and then, not bothering with the ladder, jumped into the darkness.

Sikes and Hodge dumped their chutes in as well. Closing the hatch behind them, they descended into a pitch-black tunnel via the ladder. There was only one direction to go, so they double-timed it, shoulder to shoulder, on soft-soled boots.

Valmunin was already too far ahead for them to see. The tunnel was dusty and dry and looked to be constructed using pre-fabricated culverts. It was a uniform ten feet wide and eight feet tall.

A scraping sound echoed from the darkness far ahead. It was loud in the haunting silence. A minute later, they reached a T in the tunnel. An arrow pointing to the left was scratched on the wall.

Hodge adjusted her mental map. They must have crossed under the road and were now moving toward the prison wall.

A distant, dim light revealed another T in the tunnel. The light came from the right. A hundred yards down the tunnel, they could see two dead bodies. Freshly killed vampires. Both skulls were crushed. A heavy steel door stood open. Valmunin was nowhere to be seen.

Hodge paused to remove the lanyard from the body that still had one. The guards' shotgun safeties were still on.

The nature of the walls changed just beyond the door. Concrete walls were now brick and mortar. The corridor now took a hard left and opened into a room. It looked like a break room. A table in the center, and lockers lined the side walls. This one contained six dead vampires. All their heads were caved in. Half died in their chairs. The others died worse but on their feet. And they all died quietly.

Beyond the guard room was a hallway that led left and right. To the left, an opening allowed light to flood in.

They stepped through, over a ledge a foot tall. Hodge scanned left to right as Sikes scanned right to left. It was a hidden entrance. It would have been a massive, elegant mirror on a grand staircase landing if they closed it behind them—an emergency exit.

They didn't count the number of dead in this room, more than twenty, and primarily humans. It was the worst carnage Hodge had ever seen. She avoided the expanding pools of blood like lava.

Hodge's mind flashed to that first night in the diner where she met Beck.

"He's going to kill everyone," Sikes said. Her tone was unsure of how she felt about it.

"Why did he even want us here? To follow him?" Hodge asked, and Sikes just shrugged. They started to run faster. The path of destruction was easy to follow.

***

He drank his fill. Ancient blood, thick and sweet as honey. Full of the life force of all the souls they'd consumed. His muscles hummed with it. His eyes could now see individual eyelashes across the room in complete darkness. He could hear hearts beating through stone walls.

And he could smell the ancient beings he was approaching.

Once again, he shook the gore from his Halligan just in time to face a dozen more guards. Human and vampire this time.

The humans and lesser vampires froze in their tracks at the sight of his eyes. The wave of chaos and command flowed from him. But two of the vampires were ancient. These two opened fire.

Valmunin could smell the depleted uranium. He knew he was a blur, even to them, even as his Halligan found their skulls. An instant later, they were all dead. His left hand felt the exposed bone on his face that led from his cheekbone along his skull, bisecting his left ear.

He turned to the intricately carved double doors. They were intended to swing out, but his powerful kick and crashing arms sent them both flying from the hinges.

The room was a vast, elegant bed chamber. A giant roaring fireplace and a hundred candles lit the room. It was all dark paneling, thick Persian rugs, overstuffed furniture, tables, and full bookcases.

The room seemed empty until a figure in the bed stirred.

"Rhys? Rhys Valmunin, my love. Is that really you?"

Valmunin felt the voice wash over him with the surprise of realization. It felt like a welcome. It felt like home. Inside him, the ancient Viking screamed and fought against the chains of lust and enslavement in her voice. But he knew he was helpless.

She sat up, then stood. The see-through silk she wore hid nothing as she drifted toward him. Her eyes glowed brighter than his. She was more beautiful than he remembered. Long silky black hair, delicate Asian eyes, perfect ivory skin he longed to caress again. Hundreds of years fell away. The Viking screams faded into the distance as she approached. It was the power he never had. The power of the maker. He had never made another vampire. Didn't know or remember the power of this influence.

He didn't notice when the Halligan slipped from his fingers to the carpet. When she was close enough, her hands laid on his chest, and he could feel the light go out of his eyes. Stolen by her, by Shén Xiān, just like that first night on the burning ship…

She climbed his body, pressing close until her arms were around his neck. She licked the open wound on his cheek and fondled his ruined ear. She licked her fingers as Valmunin lowered her to the bed.

He had known it might come to this.

***

Sloan watched as the chopper expertly landed on the custom flatbed trailer. The hydraulic side walls began to rise up before the rotor breaks had entirely stopped them. Two minutes later, with the help of Oddjob and a sledgehammer, the entire rotor assembly was down. A minute after that, the roof tarp slid back, and the truck was rolling.

The three vampire bodies had been transferred to a minivan that looked like it belonged to a typical family. One of the women from Shockley's team looked exactly like a soccer mom, right down to the sports equipment and folding lawn chairs piled on top of the black blanket.

The white van and Sloan's car had their plates changed back while the chopper was being secured. Drivers were changed.

The car and van would be abandoned in the Fresno Yosemite International Airport long-term parking with their original plates.

Oddjob and Sloan were in a Ford F-150 pickup that had seen better days. Oddjob did his best to look Hispanic. The Dirty John Deer hat and flannel shirt with the sleeves torn off finished the disguise. Sloan wore an equally dirty Ford logo hat and Fog Hat concert T-shirt. He handed Oddjob two cigars.

Oddjob drew a silver cutter from his jeans and prepped both cigars. He handed one to Sloan and lit his own with a torch-style lighter.

Oddjob handed the lighter to Sloan and placed a hand on the wheel so Sloan could light his cigar.

"I'm worried about Hodge. I like her," Oddjob said. "She's the one heading into the center of that shitstorm."

"That was a big diversion," Sloan said, cracking his window. "Beck will get them out."

"Shockley is a crazy bastard, but he can fly," Oddjob puffed.

"Can I ask you a question? Answer only if you can be honest," Sloan said.

"Sure, chief," Oddjob replied without hesitation.

"How long have you been feeding information to Valmunin?" Sloan asked without looking at him.

"Just over a year. It was Switch that first found him." He was honest.

"That first night in the alley, did you tell him about the operation in advance?" Sloan looked at him now.

"Yes. He said he could handle it, and none of us would be in danger," Oddjob said. "He was right."

"And the apartment building op?" Sloan asked.

"He didn't know they were hunting him. He didn't know it was a trap until then... Crash died. Part of me died that day as well." Oddjob fell silent.

***

Sikes and Hodge rounded the last corner to find broken and splattered guards in a circle. Waves of lust poured out of the broken double doors. They slowly entered the room, and the waves of ardor and raw desire became like a perfumed headwind as they pushed through.

From the bed, they heard a quiet female voice with an Asian accent. "My love, I will feed on you for weeks until all that's yours is mine," Shén Xiān said. "Unlike you, I never ran out of brethren to feed upon. I make them, they serve me, just like you will again… You were always my slave."

Valmunin was on his back in the bed, his eyes rolled back, showing only whites. She bit down hard on his neck again.

Sikes crushed broken glass underfoot.

Shén Xiān's head snapped up, and she saw them for the first time. Her mouth opened in a fang-filled scream. A clawed hand thrust out toward them, sending a flood of fear, chaos, confusion, and, most of all, a command to not move.

It washed over Hodge like a storm. But she didn't feel it. She only heard it. And she ignored it. Hodge and Sikes were both Valkyries and immune to her influence. Valmunin had known. He had always known.

"Not today, bitch," Hodge said. They both opened fire, full auto.

Round after round tore through her tiny frame. She toppled over onto the floor and actually started to get up as they reloaded. Hodge was faster to reload and halfway through her magazine when Sikes opened fire again—magazine after magazine.

Only when enough of her muscle mass had been destroyed did she stop moving. Her right cheek was gone. Most of her hair on that side was also torn away. In the candlelight, the left side of her face remained beautiful. Her eyes were still intact. Watching.

Hodge's ears were ringing as Valmunin rose and retrieved his Halligan. He stood between Sikes and Hodge.

"After you fled without me, I also escaped, my love," Shén Xiān whispered. "I followed in your wake. I watched you drink your fill from our brothers again and again. Like a hyena, feeding after the lion, I fed on them as well. I was certain you would feed on me when you discovered I was the burned husk beggar."

Hodge had heard enough. Slammed in another mag and aimed for the eyes. Valmunin stopped her.

"I fed when I could. I found that to hide, I couldn't hunt." She struggled to draw in a breath. "I became the first of our kind to… farm." She struggled even more on her next breath.

It was then that realization dawned, and Shén Xiān formed a single whispered word before the light faded from her eyes. "Valkyries… again."

***

Beck and Takashi approached Pleasant Valley from the East. Takashi drove the ambulance with all the lights flashing. A hundred police, fire, and emergency vehicles were already on the scene. They paused only a moment at the corner of the orchard. As soon as they heard the doors slam shut, they were moving again.

It was chaos on the radio. Riots had broken out on the maximum-security side. Most inmates were already in their bunks when the lockdown was initiated. There were a few small fires. There was concern that it was more than smoke and tear gas.

Beck slid open the divider, and Valmunin was on the gurney, wearing an oxygen mask. He was covered in blood—an inch-wide gash exposed bone from his cheek to his ruined ear. Hodge and Sikes no longer wore tactical vests. They sported EMT windbreakers.

No one challenged them as they left the scene.

Valmunin removed the mask. He looked up at them and slowly touched his ruined ear.

"Ouch…" he said deadpan.

"Fucking crybaby," Sikes said.

22. THE UTAH BASE

Beck and Hodge climbed out of the chopper into a bright sunny day on the oil rig, now known as Utah Base. He carried a small duffle bag only. Snow stayed to do a proper tiedown.

Utah Base had changed a lot, rapidly. By the time they'd returned from California, the base had been fully provisioned. Renovation planning had begun.

"Did I see two new air defense missile batteries up there?" Hodge asked.

"They have been busy," Beck replied. "Let's take a walk. Have a better look."

They climbed down a set of stairs so they were just below the landing pad. One of the new automated sentries was there. Beside it was an incongruous park bench bolted down facing west.

They sat there in the sun, sheltered from the wind, in silence for fifteen minutes before Hodge spoke.

"It still isn't over," she began. "I need to tell you something before I chicken out, Tim."

She never calls me Tim.

"That first night in the diner. Do you know what I was doing?" Her voice was shaking. "I was only holding on by a thread."

He had never heard her so serious or so sad.

Oh God, was she thinking of suicide?

"Doing? Besides drinking a ton of coffee?" He was trying to lighten the mood. It didn't work.

"I was praying." She swallowed hard. "I hadn't prayed since I was a kid. Even then, I never meant it. But that night, I meant it. I sat in the last booth, crying into my coffee because I had nothing left. I prayed to God to send someone to save me."

Beck looked at her then. Silent tears ran down her cheeks.

"And God sent you…" She looked into his eyes. "A priest."

He held her eyes. He wiped a tear with his thumb. "Didn't you hear? I haven't been a priest for like fifteen minutes." He gently kissed her.

Hodge half laughed, half sobbed.

"And I lied to you," he said, "I pray all the time. I prayed for strength constantly. Then I learned, to make me stronger, God set me more and more difficult tasks."

"Why do you say that?" She reached up and placed her hand on his so he wouldn't draw it away.

"The six I killed in Iraq that night, I now believe, were Stage twos. I thought at the time they were just three men and three women. Insurgents. They chased me in the dark through a camp of my dead friends, playing with me like six cats and a mouse. But I made it to the chopper fifty yards ahead of them."

"To fly out?" she presumed.

"No." He swallowed hard. "There was a 50-caliber chain gun mounted in the door on that side. I used it on them all."

They were clinging to each other now, raw in their hidden pain. Time passed as they held each other. The winds changed, and the cold winter breeze reminded them what winter would be like.

"I love you, Timothy Beck." She said it like it was a challenge as they stood.

"I love you, too, but we still have work to do today." He held up the duffel.

"So romantic," she said, but her steps were lighter.

***

They entered the mess hall, and everyone shouted "Norm" and then laughed. It never seemed to get old for them. They continued through the tables toward the Lab where Dr. Franklin now lived in isolation—seeing no one but Beeker once a day and receiving no news.

Sloan waved them over to his table. Only then did Beck recognize Valmunin and Sikes. Both were wearing glasses and lab coats and looked more like Beeker than members of an assault team. They held hands. Valmunin was gently caressing her hand.

Beck knew it was an illusion. Hodge was immune to it, as was Sikes.

"Beck, I'd like you to meet Valin Miller and Pamala Sikes, the newest members of your team," Sloan said.

"My team, sir?" Beck asked.

"It was Hodge's idea," Sloan said. "I think she was getting sick of fetching your coffee and wanted help," Sloan joked.

"Just a few more loose cannons," Hodge added.

"Were you really a priest five minutes ago?" Sikes added.

"Sloan and I have made a deal," Valin said in a voice completely human. "I will help you weed out the remaining farms and clean up the other teams, and we won't try to kill each other."

"How does Sloan really know if you can be trusted?" Beck asked. "All you need do is say 'Trust me,' and we cannot do otherwise. No offense."

"That may work on him and you, but not them." Val gestured at Sikes and Hodge. "They would know."

***

"Good afternoon, Dr. Franklin. We didn't mean to ignore you so much for the last week. I see Beeker has made you more comfortable in your isolation. Nice TV, a sofa there, even a bed. A hospital bed, but better than nothing."

Beck set the duffle on the stainless autopsy table between them. I wanted to introduce you to the new team members you'll be working with.

Hodge opened the door.

"I'd like you to meet Pamala Sikes and our newest recruit, Valin Miller." She didn't recognize him.

Beck opened the duffle and drew out a head by its long black hair. He set it on the table facing her. Franklin recognized her at once.

"She told us a lot about you and others. And once too often, we had to ask her twice," Beck lied. "At least we know now that if the collar worked on her, it would work on you."

Franklin was backing away but soon had nowhere to go.

"We know you worked at the prison. We know you made vampires for her from the worst inmates in the supermax solitary confinement and fed them for years until she was ready to harvest them."

There was a line spray painted on the floor. It was the detonation point. She knew it. No one ever crossed it until now.

Valin crossed the line and slowly approached her. As he did, he changed from a simple man to the monster Rhys Valmunin.

"Todd Sanders sends his regards. He tells us you worked

together at Pleasant Valley. He has also told us the names of the other docs placed on other crews. You'll also tell me to see if he is lying." Valmunin used the voice. It washed over her like a tsunami.

Franklin fell on her ass. Her scream could be heard in the mess hall. The Valkyries laughed, knowing now that their eyes glowed as the voice washed over them.

AFTERWARD

In the spring of 2022, I was clearing out several dozen hard drives from my office. It was an entire box of drives that had come from every computer I had ever owned. I was copying files from the old drives to a single big one. All the photos, music, videos, and documents were getting consolidated into one place. In these files, I found the outline of this book, dated March 1993.

I find this to be very satisfying to finish this book 30 years later.

It was a departure from my usual science fiction novels. And I have already begun an outline of Book 2, titled currently as *Blood Sky Dreams*. But I already have a couple of other projects nearing completion. It is queued up for my Spring 2024 Writer Retreat.

Martin Wilsey
Fredericksburg, VA
October 31, 2023

MARTIN WILSEY

BLOOD SKY DREAMS

The Vampire Conspiracy

Book 2

ABOUT THE AUTHOR

Martin Wilsey is a full-time author and creator of the bestselling *Solstice 31 Saga.*

Mr. Wilsey's first novel, *Still Falling,* was published on March 31st of 2015. Less than three years and over half a million published words later, he retired from his career as a research scientist for a government-funded think tank. As a full-time science fiction writer, Mr. Wilsey still uses his research and whiteboard skills to keep the books flowing. He likes to put the science back into science fiction.

Mr. Wilsey has more projects than he has time. So please feel free to email him and distract him even more.

He and his wife, Brenda, live in Virginia with their pets, Whiskey, Brandy, and Bailey.

Email him or follow him on social media!

He just might kill you in his next novel...

```
https://linktr.ee/wilsey
martin.wilsey@gmail.com
```

ACKNOWLEDGMENTS

This book will be published in the winter of 2023, thirty years after it began. It was a fun ride.

It has been another weird year for me personally. There were too many funerals and not enough weddings. I also had a heart attack over the summer. There's nothing like dancing on the edge of the abyss to change your priorities.

Many people have helped and encouraged me with this book. I'll list some here with my thanks: Stephanie Mirro, Erica Gravely, Kelly Lenz Carr, Joe Kirk, Ron Jennings, Marcy Abrams, David Keener, Shea Mcgale, Lea Jones, Rob Metzler, Marti Hoffman, Mike Plummer, and Tricia Sloan.

I also need to thank the Loudoun Science Fiction and Fantasy Writers Group, aka The Hourlings, for helping me become a better writer and distracting me with projects I can't resist.

A special thanks to my wife, Brenda, for all the help and support she brings me.

I must also thank, as usual, my cat, Bailey. He doesn't care if I ever sell another book as long as the sun shines on his window seat as I write.

I also have a new dog named Whiskey. She'll keep me walking. Maybe she'll find her way into one of my novels in the future.

Coming Soon from Martin Wilsey

9 798889 719032 4